HORROR HEIGHTS

NOW
LIVESCREAMING

Close one eye and tilt the top of the book away from you to read the hidden message.

BEC HILL

HORROR HEIGHTS

NOW LIVESCREAMING

ILLUSTRATIONS
by BERAT
PEKMEZCI

HODDER

HODDER CHILDREN'S BOOKS

First published in Great Britain in 2022 by Hodder & Stoughton

1 3 5 7 9 10 8 6 4 2

Text copyright © Bec Hill, 2022
Illustrations copyright © Berat Pekmezci, 2022
Map copyright © Tom Crowley, 2021, adapted from a map by Berat Pekmezci.

The moral rights of the author and illustrators have been asserted.

A CIP catalogue record for this book is available from the
British Library.

ISBN 978 1 444 96234 5

Typeset in Sassoon Infant by Avon DataSet Ltd, Arden Road,
Alcester, Warwickshire

Printed and bound in Great Britain by Clays Ltd, Elcograf S.p.A.

The paper and board used in this book
are made from wood from responsible sources.

Hodder Children's Books
An imprint of
Hachette Children's Group
Part of Hodder & Stoughton Limited
Carmelite House
50 Victoria Embankment
London EC4Y 0DZ

An Hachette UK Company
www.hachette.co.uk

www.hachettechildrens.co.uk

A NOTE FROM THE AUTHOR

In my travels around the world as a writer, comedian and TV presenter, I've heard my fair share of spooky stories and strange happenings. Every town, neighbourhood, or community has one. But one place in particular stood out from the rest. It didn't have one unexplained event — it had THIRTEEN. Weirder still, they all occurred between the SAME dates *and* to individuals at the SAME school. I have been fortunate enough to be granted access to classified reports and exclusive interviews with the people involved so that their experiences can be anonymously shared without affecting any current investigations.

For the purposes of privacy and safety, names have been changed and I have dubbed the location "Horror Heights". If any of the incidents mentioned within these books have happened to you, or if you believe you might live in "Horror Heights", please report it to an adult you trust. Stay safe and remember: *you don't have to give the subs what they want …*

Bec Hill

SPORTS
CENTRE

SCHOOL

RYAN'S HOME

FRIDAY

CHAPTER 1

"LOOK OUT!!!"

Before Ryan had a chance to look up, his best friend, Ishaan, shunted him off the footpath.

"What???" said Ryan, looking around startled.

"You nearly stepped in THAT!" Ishaan pointed at a MASSIVE dog poo.

"Oh, whoa! Close call! Thanks, Ish." Ryan angled his phone at the colossal bum-bomb by his foot. "Hey, everyone! Check out the size of this thing!"

Ryan's handful of viewers were suitably impressed.

@r3n_brite: :-O That dog must be HUGE!!!

@seaniebee: or at least its butt is huge lololol

"Do you have to do that livestream NOW?" said Ishaan.

"Livestreams are always 'now'. They're LIVE!" Ryan quipped.

"You know what I mean," grumbled Ishaan. "It's not even 9 a.m.!"

"It's 5 o'clock somewhere," Ryan said, quoting a t-shirt his mum always wore on holiday. "And when my channel is as popular as Grimmf's, it's the Three Fs, baby!!! Fame, fun, and freebies!"

Ryan had recently started streaming whenever he could, so he could grow his fanbase. He only had about ten subscribers and his favourite streamer, Grimmf, had hundreds of thousands, but he knew if he worked hard enough, one day HIS life would be JUST as exciting!

"That's all you ever talk about these days! It's all my channel this, and Grimmf that. You need to snap out of it, brud. At least while we're walking to school!" said Ishaan. "Focus on what's in front of you!"

"You should listen to your bud," said a familiar voice behind Ryan. "Focus on what's in front of you!"

Like a gust of wind, Ryan's older sister launched him towards the monstrous mound of pavement poop – only to pull him back to safety at the very last minute.

"LILY!!!" Ryan huffed.

"RYAN!!" she echoed in her whiniest voice.

"You're so lucky you're an only child," Ryan said to Ishaan. Then he turned to Lily. "And it's BRUD, not bud! Because we're buds – but also, we're close like brothers. Y'know?" Ryan clasped his hands together to illustrate his point. "Bruds."

Lily stared back stone-faced, as Ryan stood awkwardly holding his own hands.

"Whatever!" said Lily. She called over her shoulder as she power-walked ahead, "Pull your trousers up, I can see your undies!"

Ryan tugged at his trousers indignantly and switched his attention back to his phone.

"Sorry about that! My sister has NO respect for the stream! Maybe I should do this later?"

Ishaan read the comments over Ryan's shoulder. "Nooo, not another prank, please?"

"But I made THIS!" Ryan said, pulling something out of his pocket.

It was a plastic spider tied to a hair clip with fishing line.

Ishaan wrinkled his nose. "You don't have to try so hard. Chill it with the pranks – Mo's not been the same since his birthday sleepover!"

Ryan chuckled at the memory. One of his subscribers had suggested he put his friend Mo's hand in a bowl of warm water while everyone was asleep, and it had ended rather hilariously.

"I gained a sub from that stream!"

"Yeah, but I think you LOST us a friend," Ishaan said, unamused. "Dunno about you, but I'd like to have some mates left by the time we start high school next year."

"By the time we start high school, I'll be so rich and famous, EVERYONE will want to be our friend!"

Ishaan rolled his eyes, which silently meant, It's YOUR funeral!

Ryan responded with a lopsided grin, as if to say, I know what I'm doing!

(The pair were so close that sometimes they had entire conversations without saying a single word.)

He sprinted up behind his sister and slipped the clip into her hair.

"Whoa! Lily! Something just fell out of that tree on to your head!" said Ryan.

"Huh?" As his sister spun around to face him, the

fake spider swung from the hairclip and dangled by her nose, like an abseiler taking a break on Mt Rushmore.

"AAAHHHHHHHHH! GET IT OFF! GET IT OFF!" she screamed, shaking her head upside-down.

Ryan struggled to hold his phone steady as he laughed.

> **@CUPCAKECASS:** she looks like the lead singer of a death metal band XD
>
> **@hamsterking999:** This is the content I came here for!
>
> **@perrywinklethe2nd:** SUBBED!

Discovering the spider was fake, Lily yanked the clip out of her hair and threw it at him.

He caught it before it hit his face. "Hey! That could've blinded me! Now smile! You're on air!"

"YOU DID THIS FOR YOUR STUPID CHANNEL?!" Lily roared.

Ryan ended the stream and slipped his phone into

his pocket as Lily made a grab for it.

"Gotta give the subs what they want!" he said with a shrug.

"I'll give YOU something!" Lily seethed.

Ryan braced himself. He knew what Lily was going to give him.

And it wasn't a present.

CHAPTER 2

Lily hooked her arm around Ryan's neck and gave him a noogie. It was always impossible for him to escape her headlocks. She was three-and-a-half years older than him, which also made her three-and-a-half years taller AND three-and-a-half years stronger.

Ishaan watched from a safe distance and attempted to stifle his giggles.

"What are you?" Lily hissed.

"Mum said you're not allowed to use your karate on me!" Ryan moaned as he tried to wriggle free of her vice-like grip.

"I SAID, what are you?"

"Ow! You're hurting me!" he whined. (She wasn't, but sometimes it was enough to get her to stop.)

"I'll let go if you tell me what you are!"

They hadn't reached the main road yet, so the chances of someone else seeing them and stopping her were slim. Ryan groaned. His sister was the WORST! He had no other choice than to give in …

"I'm a smelly little egg," he whimpered.

"Sorry, what's that?" Lily asked. "Speak up."

"I'M A SMELLY LITTLE EGG!"

Lily released Ryan from the headlock, but before he could make a run for it, she grabbed the waistband of his underpants. He froze, fearing any movement might result in a self-wedgie.

"You'll PAY for that prank," she said in a whisper so threatening, it seemed to make the sun hide behind the clouds.

She let go and Ryan bolted around the corner with Ishaan close behind. They crossed the main road which separated their school from the high school, so Lily wouldn't follow them. He also pulled his trousers up over his undies (just to be safe).

"Why didn't you help me back there?" Ryan asked.

"I did! I told you not to prank her! But did you listen to me?"

Ryan chose not to dignify the question with a response.

It was an otherwise lovely morning. Despite the traffic zooming noisily past on their right, the birds could still be heard singing in the park on their left. The school loomed up ahead of them and horns tooted goodbye as parents waved at their children through their car windows before driving off.

Ryan eventually spoke. "JD said their uncle won an Aston Martin Vulcan. Imagine if they got dropped off to school in THAT beast!"

Ishaan snorted. "Yeah RIGHT! Didn't JD also say their uncle won a Phene?"

A viral video depicting an indestructible phone made from graphene had been doing the rounds online.

The Phene was meant to be the thinnest, lightest, and most flexible phone ever invented — except no one knew where or how to buy one.

"Yeah! I didn't even know it had been released!" said Ryan.

"That's because it hasn't! It doesn't exist! The video was a hoax!" said Ishaan.

Ryan looked dejected. "Ahhh, butts. I shoulda known it was fake news."

They both saw Lily make a dash for the high school gates on the other side of the road. Ryan checked his watch.

He looked at Ishaan with panic in his eyes. *We're late!*

Ishaan mirrored his expression. *Ms Strapp will kill us!*

Their strict teacher, Ms Strapp, struck fear into the hearts of even the bravest of souls. Legend said she used to teach at a prison, but that she'd been forced to leave because the inmates found her too intimidating.

The school bell rang and without saying a word, the pair broke into a sprint.

Ms Strapp was closing the door to their classroom when they burst into the building.

She spotted them and bellowed, "RYAN! ISHAAN! YOU'VE GOT FIVE SECONDS! FIVE ... FOUR ..."

They raced down the hall towards her.

"DON'T RUN IN THE HALL!" she shouted.

Ishaan switched to a stride.

Ryan skidded to a halt. "How are we supposed to ..."

Ms Strapp ignored Ryan and continued counting down. "THREE ... TWO ..."

Without hesitation, Ishaan leaned backwards, grabbed Ryan by the arm and swung him into the room.

"... ONE," said their teacher as she shut the door behind them.

CHAPTER 3

"That was EPIC!" Ryan declared.

He and Ishaan were discussing their heroic arrival as they walked to their usual spot near the shady apple tree at lunch. The grassy mound had a nice view of the park next to the school and was quieter than the benches by the basketball hoops where their classmates hung out.

Ryan continued excitedly. "Ms Strapp was SO close to locking me out! I felt like Indiana Jones when he escapes from that giant boulder!"

Ishaan laughed. "Yeah, but I'M the one who saved you! So that makes ME Indiana Jones!"

Ryan pretended to look offended. "Then what does that make me?"

"Indiana Jones's ... hat?" Ishaan teased.

"Well, if I'M a hat, then I guess you should

WEAR me!" Ryan attempted to climb up on to Ishaan's shoulders.

"Ahh! Ryan! Get off! This isn't parkour! You're too heavy!" giggled Ishaan.

"I'm not too heavy! I'm a hat! Put me on your head!"

"All right! All right! You're not a hat!"

Ryan dismounted and grinned. "And don't you forget it!"

They sat down and opened their lunchboxes. Ryan was about to bite into his sandwich when his phone buzzed with a notification:

@GrimmfOfficial is now livestreaming.

Ryan followed the link and Grimmf appeared, sporting their signature Grimmf-branded tracksuit and their classic charismatic grin. The only thing whiter than their teeth was the studio they were standing in. If it weren't for the slightly visible edges where the walls, ceiling and floor met, it would have looked like the room went on for ever.

"Hi, Grimmions! It's me! The one-and-only Grimmf!" announced the streamer.

Ishaan sighed. "Imagine being THAT happy ALL the time! It'd be exhausting!"

"Uh, you mean it'd be AMAZING!" scoffed Ryan.

"Can we watch something else instead? I'm bored of watching Grimmf every lunch."

"BORED!?" said Ryan. "Grimmf is NEVER boring! Remember when they played Ultimate Crime Spree IV non-stop for TWO days? Or when they did that series of makeup tutorials? Or how they taught basic coding the other week? Name another streamer with THAT much range. I'll wait."

Ishaan held his hands up in surrender.

"Okay, Grimmions! You know the drill! Tell me what you want and we'll see what arrives!" said Grimmf.

Anyone who subscribed to Grimmf was able to make a request in the chat room. All they had to do was type "I want …" followed by whatever item they wanted to see Grimmf play with. The most popular requests would appear – almost instantaneously – from the walls. It was Ryan's favourite part about Grimmf's streams.

"This bit is all rigged, you know," said Ishaan through a handful of grapes. "Grimmf programs bots to ask for whatever products their sponsors want advertised. That's why everything arrives so quickly. The walls are pre-loaded."

"Nah. Grimmf would never use fake accounts. The subscribers and requests are all legit," said Ryan. "I bet if we ask for something, it shows up."

"Bet your lunch?" asked Ishaan.

"Sure," said Ryan. He shook Ishaan's hand. "What should we ask for?"

Ishaan shrugged. "I dunno … a chainsaw?"

Ryan joined the chat room.

@ryanlols: I want a chainsaw!

The request was immediately buried by thousands of other "I want …" messages from Grimmf's extensive fanbase.

"Hopefully enough people see our request and ask for the same thing to get it trending," said Ryan.

The comments in the chat room continued to zip up the screen until a high-pitched tone sharply rang.

DING!

"Okay! What have we got?" said Grimmf, rubbing their hands with delight.

Doors of all sizes swung open from the walls, revealing compartments containing a wealth of goodies.

"No way! A scooter!" said Grimmf as they retrieved a Yamaha R1 from a recess in the back wall. "I'm kidding! I know it's a motorbicycle!"

More gifts emerged — but no chainsaw.

Ishaan shot Ryan a look which said, I told you so!

"That doesn't prove you're right! It just means it wasn't requested by enough people!" said Ryan. He gripped his sandwich tightly.

Ishaan was unconvinced. "Mmm-hmm." He held out his hand.

Ryan groaned and handed over his lunch.

"The best-tasting sandwiches are the ones you win!" Ishaan gloated as he took a bite. Then he promptly spat it on to his lap. "Except for this one! This is the WORST-tasting sandwich!"

Ryan felt like he'd dodged a bullet.

"It tastes like egg and ... strawberry yoghurt!" Ishaan spluttered. He inspected the filling. "Aw, gross! It IS egg and strawberry yoghurt! Try it! It's rank!"

"No thanks!" said Ryan. "Must be one of Dad's experimental recipes."

Ishaan held the sandwich out. "Bruds-for-life suffer together!"

Ryan gave in and nibbled a corner. "EW! That is NASTY! I think there's pesto in it too!"

"I hope so! Otherwise this bread is mooouuuldy!" said Ishaan as he chucked the sandwich into a nearby bin.

"I wish I'd streamed our reactions! Subs love that sort of stuff!" said Ryan.

"Not everything has to be content, Ryan," said Ishaan. "Even Grimmf takes breaks."

"Only little ones. I don't think they go to bed," said Ryan.

Ishaan studied Grimmf's flawless complexion on Ryan's phone. "They must be wearing a lot of makeup. They don't LOOK like someone who doesn't go to bed …"

"Yeah, but Mum says no one looks tired until they hit thirty."

Ishaan shared his less-daring peanut butter sandwich with Ryan as they tried to guess exactly how old Grimmf was. Ryan had always assumed Grimmf was just a bit older than Lily, but Ishaan pointed out that their channel had been going for three years and they didn't seem to go to school.

"Maybe there aren't any high schools where they live?" Ryan wondered aloud.

"Sounds like a nice place. Maybe we should move there next year so we don't have to go to high school either," joked Ishaan.

Ryan was about to agree when he burped. His face contorted in disgust. "I can still taste the egg and yoghurt …"

"BRUD!"

Ryan tried to waft away the belch. "Sorry! I didn't realise it was gonna stink so bad!"

"No, brud! LOOK!" Ishaan gestured at Ryan's phone.

"WHOA!!!"

Grimmf was brandishing a chainsaw.

"What a coincidence!" said Ishaan.

"Ish, that's not a coincidence! It's because we asked for it!" said Ryan.

The bell marking the end of lunch rang.

"Agree to disagree," said Ishaan as he packed up his bag. "Come on, we'd better go. I don't fancy taking my chances being late again."

Ryan groaned. "Fine."

Ishaan hummed quietly as they headed back to class.

"Is that the theme from Indiana Jones?" asked Ryan.

"Yeah," said Ishaan.

"Nice."

CHAPTER 4

As Ryan and Ishaan walked along the main road from school, the goodbye-beeps from various drivers gave way to the sound of people playing in the park. Once they were at a distance where their teacher couldn't somehow overhear them, the pair began to complain.

"I can't believe Ms Strapp gave us homework — on a FRIDAY! None of the other classes have to make stupid posters about ancient Egypt on the weekend!" Ryan ranted.

"Well, I can't believe that YOU put that fake spider in Yasue's hair — IN CLASS!" said Ishaan.

"Relax! I would never stream if Ms Strapp was there!"

"She'd only stepped out for a second! If she'd caught you, your phone would be in the Confiscation Cupboard right now with all of Connie's banned tubs of slime!"

Ryan winced at the thought of losing his phone.

A low rumbling disrupted their conversation as they crossed the main road.

"Oh, it's your belly!!!" said Ishaan. "I thought a car was coming, or something!"

"Yeah, I think it knows it's pizza night tonight," Ryan said, patting his stomach.

Lily worked at a local takeaway called Pizza Cake after school on Mondays and Fridays, so every Friday night, she brought home pizza for dinner. It was one of the few good things about having her as a sister.

"OH NO!" Ishaan grabbed Ryan by the shoulders.

"What? WHAT?!"

"Lily said she was gonna make you pay for the prank you pulled earlier! And now she's in charge of your dinner!!!"

Ryan looked concerned. "You think she might not let me have any pizza?"

"Worse! What if she puts something ON your pizza?" said Ishaan.

The colour drained from Ryan's face. "Like a cricket?"

"I was thinking of something scarier. Like poison ... or razor blades ... or ..."

"... LOTS of crickets?" said Ryan.

"Um ... Sure? But crickets ARE edible, so I don't think they're the WORST thing you could find on a pizza ..." said Ishaan. He stopped walking and gasped, "... Unless you're secretly scared of crickets???"

Ryan laughed nervously. "Hah! Crickets?! No! I'M not scared of crickets! I thought YOU were scared of crickets! That's why I said it!"

The truth was, Ryan WAS secretly scared of crickets — ever since a terrifying encounter with one thanks to his sister. But the experience had been too humiliating to share — even with his best friend. Ryan had agreed not to tell on Lily for messing with him, as long as she promised not to tell a single soul.

Ishaan raised an eyebrow. "You're lying."

"No I'm not!" Ryan lied.

"Okay then! Get ready for The Stare!"

The Stare was Ishaan's superpower. There was something about his eyes which made it impossible for people to hold his gaze if they were lying. His ability was so strong, sometimes he did it without even realising. Once, Ishaan made direct eye contact with his mum for too long and she ended up confessing what she'd got him for his birthday.

Ishaan's eyes were as sharp as fingernails and they picked at Ryan's lie like a scab. As much as Ryan tried, he couldn't withstand The Stare.

"FINE! I'm scared of crickets!" he blurted.

"I knew it! Why? Since when??" Ishaan buzzed.

"Don't make me talk about it," Ryan said quietly.

Ishaan studied Ryan's pained expression. "Whoa …

That bad, eh? Okay, you don't have to tell me right now."

Ryan gave a little relieved smile. "Thanks."

"Do you wanna come to mine and stay for dinner, then? Pretty sure Mum isn't making anything with crickets in it …"

Ryan chuckled. "Soz. I promised my subs I'd be online at 4 p.m."

After his stream that morning, he was up to fifteen subscribers. It wasn't much, but it was better than most kids his age. Ryan's classmates weren't into livestreams – or at least, they weren't into HIS livestreams – so he had to rely on strangers stumbling across his channel to build his audience.

"I'm sure your fans will understand if you miss ONE session," said Ishaan.

Ryan shook his head. "Remember when we went camping last month?"

Ishaan pretended to think deeply. "Uh, yeah. I

THINK I remember when we went camping for my BIRTHDAY."

"Right, yeah, of course! So you remember how I couldn't stream because there wasn't any signal?"

"Yeah, brud. You whinged about it all weekend. You were convinced you'd lose your subs if you didn't stream for two days."

"I DID lose subs! Tomato Mic hasn't tuned in ONCE since your birthday! That's …" Ryan did the maths in his head. "Thirty-three days. THIRTY-THREE DAYS, ISH!"

Ishaan looked puzzled. "Sorry – 'Tomato Mic'? Who's that?"

"Someone called Mic who likes tomatoes, I guess? 'Tomato Mic' was their username. I dunno where they were from, but they used to watch EVERY stream and now they don't watch me at all!"

Ishaan closed his eyes. "So let me get this straight. You're upset because someone you don't even know that well stopped watching your channel when you went camping. With me. For my birthday."

"Well, it sounds BAD if you say it like that!" said Ryan.

"That's because it IS bad! You're meant to be my brud-for-life!"

"I AM your brud-for-life!"

Ishaan shook his head. "Nah. A brud wouldn't ditch me for a bunch of randos on the internet."

Ryan was shocked. "What's your problem with fame, fun and freebies?"

"I don't HAVE a problem with it, as long as you don't forget about the Fourth F: friends!"

"Didn't realise you were such a big Ross and Rachel fan," Ryan joked.

Ishaan didn't laugh. "I'm serious. It should always be bruds before subs."

Bitterness rose from the pit of Ryan's stomach – and it wasn't due to the egg and yoghurt sandwich. Ryan's brud was supposed to support his dream, but for some reason Ishaan was intent on making him feel guilty about the work he was putting in to achieve it.

"You're just jealous because I'M gonna be the next Grimmf," muttered Ryan.

"You know what? I AM jealous!" said Ishaan. "But not of YOU. I'm jealous of your FOLLOWERS! At least you listen to THEM!"

"I listen to you ALL the TIME!" Ryan said, defensively.

"No you don't, Ry. If you listened to me as much as you listened to your subscribers, then you wouldn't be in such a big mess right now!" Ishaan said as he stormed away.

Ryan went to follow him. "What big mess?!"

Ryan looked down to see he'd stepped in a massive dog poo – the SAME massive dog poo he'd avoided that morning.

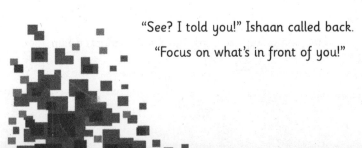

"See? I told you!" Ishaan called back. "Focus on what's in front of you!"

CHAPTER 5

"NOW can I come in?" Ryan pleaded.

He was standing on the concrete step outside his front door in his socks. Despite having scrubbed his shoe with a toothbrush for nearly an hour, he could still smell the dog poo. And so could his dad, who was standing in the doorway.

"You must have got some on your clothes while you were cleaning your shoes," Ryan's dad said nasally through his pinched nose. "Better take them off so I can pop them in the washing machine."

"What, here?" Ryan gestured at his less-than-private surroundings.

Ryan's dad looked around. "No, I suppose the neighbours don't want to see your unmentionables ... All right, come in."

Ryan took a step forward, but his dad blocked him

like a security guard at a nightclub.

"Ah-ah! The shoes stay out here. And wash that toothbrush before you throw it out. The bin smells bad enough as it is!"

Ryan left his shoes outside and headed upstairs, toothbrush in hand.

Thud. Thud. Thud.

"Ry, don't drag your bag like that!" moaned his dad.

Ryan hoisted his bag up with his spare hand and stomped the rest of the way. Without his shoes on, it didn't have the same effect.

He USED to have the house to himself on Monday and Friday afternoons while his parents and sister were at work. THEN his dad decided to do a part-time online university course on those exact days and Ryan lost his only moments of freedom.

He softly marched into the bathroom across the small landing at the top of the stairs and left the toothbrush in the sink to wash later.

Next to the bathroom was the biggest bedroom in the house – Ryan's parents' room (they even had their own TV). Sometimes his mum complained because it was above the kitchen, so it stank whenever they had fish, but as much as Ryan offered, his parents were never willing to swap.

At the other end of the landing was the second-biggest bedroom in the house – Lily's room. It was above the dining room, which his parents had converted into a home office because everyone always ate in the kitchen or the lounge. As a result, Lily's room had the best Wi-Fi signal of all the bedrooms, which Ryan found infuriating because he used the internet WAY more.

Opposite his sister's room, with a "DANGER: KEEP OUT (That means YOU, Lily!)" sign stuck to the door, was the smallest bedroom in the house – Ryan's room. (It was SO small, it was barely a bedroom in his opinion.) It had JUST enough room for a desk, a single bed, and a tiny window. When the house had been renovated a few years earlier, his parents had a built-in mirrored wardrobe installed along the wall, thinking it would stop Ryan from piling his clothes on the floor and make the room look bigger. Instead, it just reduced his floorspace by a third, which meant that his cream-coloured carpet had gone from being partially covered in clothes, to ENTIRELY covered in clothes.

Ryan entered his baby-blue (and baby-sized) room. He dumped his bag on some t-shirts, and quickly got changed into the freshest-smelling hoodie and trackpants he could find. He was running late for his afternoon livestream and didn't want to waste any more time, so he bolted to the top of the stairs.

"Here you go, Dad!!!!" he called, as he chucked the clothes down.

His dad came out of the lounge and frowned at the stinky clothing scattering the entrance.

"You couldn't go down thirteen steps to pass these to me in person?" he grumbled as he collected Ryan's clothes off the floor.

"Saves me from going UP thirteen steps again!" said Ryan, cheekily.

"Keep talking like that and there'll be no pizza for you tonight, young man!" his dad warned.

A shiver ran down Ryan's spine as the image of a cricket-covered revenge pizza flashed before his eyes.

"Um, actually, can I have nuggets or something? I feel like a change," he said.

His dad's grumpiness vanished instantly. "Wow, I'm impressed! I never thought I'd hear you turn down pizza! I might skip the pizza too – we have been having it a lot. Leave it to me and I'll sort out a tasty alternative for both of us!"

"Thanks, Dad!" Ryan yelled as he raced back to his room.

With any luck, his followers would still be online.

CHAPTER 6

Much to Ryan's relief, thirteen of his subscribers were still online. The only two missing were Ishaan and Tomato Mic, but he hadn't expected to see either of them, anyway.

He angled his screen so that the webcam wasn't pointing up his nose – something he was pretty sure Grimmf never had to do. He didn't know what streaming equipment they used, but it definitely wasn't their big sister's hand-me-down laptop. Still, it was better than his phone.

"Hey, cheesebutts! Ryan-lols here!" he announced as he went live.

@ALL_HAIL_KING_ROB: finally!

@imagoblin: w00t w00t!

@stevem: we've been waiting 4 aaaagesssss!

"Aw, sorry, Stevem!"

@stevem: it's STEVE M not STEVEM!

"Serious? I've been calling you Stevem this whole time!" he chuckled.

@007JamesBinned: Why're you late?

"I stepped in that dog poop from this morning!"

@r3n_brite: bahaha wish I'd seen that!

@DrkR00m: sucks 2 b u!

@CUPCAKECASS: the same 1?! im dying XD

Ryan grinned. "Yeah it was rank! I coulda started my stream earlier on my phone, but I figured there wasn't much demand to see me clean poo off my shoe!"

@ALL_HAIL_KING_ROB: What did you clean it with?

@CUPCAKECASS: hope it wasn't ur hands! 55555

@hamsterking999: His tongue ;-)

"Hang on, I'll show you!"

Ryan dashed to the bathroom and returned with

the putrid, poopy toothbrush to show his audience.

@BilalZCakes: that's the last time I lend u my toothbrush!

@seaniebee: lololololol

@Sonic_Sooz: more like a POOPbrush amiright?

A whiff of dog poo and disinfectant wafted up Ryan's nostrils and made him gag.

"Okay, I'ma get rid of this before I vom!"

@stevem: brush ur teeth with it!

"Shut up, Stevem – I mean Steve!" Ryan laughed.

But he wasn't laughing for long.

@din0mite: omgosh yesss!!! u gotta give the subs what they want @ryanlols!

@CUPCAKECASS: Do it! Give us what we want! XD

@hamsterking999: This is the content I came here for!

Soon they were all urging him to brush his teeth with the poopbrush.

"No way! I don't wanna get sick!" said Ryan.

@hamsterking999: booo

@din0mite: boring! bye!

@perrywinklethe2nd: UNSUBBED

Ryan's followers suddenly dropped to eleven. Then six. Until all he had left were two. Which was the same as having NONE, unless Ishaan and Tomato Mic both decided to start watching his streams again.

He stared at the empty chat room in stunned silence. It'd taken him MONTHS to reach fifteen subscribers, but because he didn't give them what they wanted, he'd lost them within SECONDS.

CHAPTER 7

By the time his mum and sister got home, Ryan was still streaming to no one.

He had been waiting online in case his followers returned – he'd even held on to the poopbrush in case he could convince them to re-subscribe if he put it in his mouth – but none of them came back.

A few new people tuned in when he started playing Danger Universe (an online multiplayer game also known as "DaVerse"), but he kept getting chopped in half by another player who was running around with an axe, so the viewers got bored and stopped watching.

"RYAN! DINNER!" yelled his dad from downstairs.

Defeated, he ended the stream and took the unwashed toothbrush back to the bathroom sink. Then he moped down the stairs and slunk into the kitchen.

His mum and Lily were already sitting at the

round family table, while his dad was crouched by the dishwasher, trying to decipher which of the plates were dirty and which ones were clean. As Ryan took a seat across from his mum, Lily's phone vibrated against her empty glass, making it sound like a tiny school bell. She reached over to check it.

"No screens at the table!" their mum screeched.

Ryan thought it was a stupid rule. On weekends, they were allowed to eat on the couch in the living room, but the rest of the time, they all had to awkwardly face each other at the kitchen table. He wondered if Grimmf had to eat with their family. He couldn't recall ever seeing Grimmf's family. Or seeing Grimmf eat, for that matter. Ryan envied Grimmf for living alone and being able to eat whatever, whenever and wherever they wanted.

The mouth-watering scent of melted cheese coming from the pizza box in the middle of the table was almost good enough to take Ryan's mind off the horrific day he'd had. But just as he was about to take a slice, Lily batted his hand away.

"This is for me and Mum! Dad said you didn't want pizza tonight!" she said.

The pizza had smelled so enticing, Ryan had completely forgotten that he'd asked for nuggets instead.

"Here's OUR dinner, Ry!" said his dad, proudly presenting a steaming bowl of green slop.

"This isn't nuggets!" said Ryan, horrified.

His dad laughed. "Obviously! I thought you didn't want pizza because you were trying to be healthy, so I whipped THIS up! My own recipe — spinach and kale stew. MUCH better than nuggets!"

Dark-green lumps bobbed about in a bright, runny green goo. The sight of it made Ryan want to vomit — in fact, it looked like he already had.

"Dig in!" said his dad.

Everyone started tucking into their meals except Ryan.

He was too angry. He was down to one subscriber and was being forced to eat something which resembled an ogre's snot.

And it was ALL Ishaan's fault! If Ishaan had stopped him from stepping in dog poo, he would have been gaming for his subs at 4 p.m. and not scrubbing poop off his shoes with a toothbrush. And if Ishaan hadn't suggested that Lily might sabotage his dinner, he would've been feasting on cheese-laden pizza and not staring at his dad's disgusting stew.

His leg jiggled with fury as he typed a message to Ishaan on his phone under the table.

> You ruined my life! You're dead to me.

Just as he pressed send, his phone was whipped out of his hands by his sister. She passed it to their mum, who glared at Ryan.

"NO SCREENS AT THE TABLE!" she repeated, sternly.

"Okay! I'll keep it in my pocket. Give it back," Ryan said with his hand outstretched.

His mum gripped the phone with a sly smile. "Y'know, Ryan ... I need a volunteer at the tournament on Sunday. One of the parents who was going to assist on the day has twisted his ankle."

Every year, there was a Horror Heights Community Tournament at the sports centre where Ryan's mum worked. Local residents competed against one another in various events, regardless of their age. It was a fun way for everyone in the area to socialise – that is, everyone except Ryan and Lily. If they ever went to watch, their mum always roped them into helping, so they had stopped going.

"I can't! I lost all my subs today, so now I have to stream ALL weekend to get my numbers back up!" he wailed.

"You won't get many views, Ry. Most of your classmates will be at the tournament!" said his mum.

"Nooo! They don't watch me anyway! They're

more into influencers and YouTubers," Ryan explained.

His parents exchanged concerned glances.

"Who watches your channel then, Ryan?" asked his dad.

"I dunno! Just people from wherever who like what I do!"

His mum spoke through gritted teeth. "You've been letting STRANGERS watch you stream from your bedroom??"

"AND sometimes when he walks to school!" Lily added.

Ryan shot her a dirty look.

"Right, well, I'm putting a stop to THAT!" said his mum, as she swiped and tapped the screen.

"What're you doing with my phone??" he cried.

"I'm putting a parental lock on your channel so no one can watch or subscribe to it without my approval first."

"NOOOOOOOOO!!!" screamed Ryan.

He instantly regretted not setting a facial recognition lock on his phone, like he'd done with his laptop. There was NO WAY he could EVER become the next Grimmf if his mum restricted who could watch his livestreams!

He tried to snatch the phone from his mother's fingers by lunging over the table, but she pulled it out of his reach. He lost balance and belly-flopped on to the pizza.

The pizza's greasy sauce seeped through Ryan's hoodie and smooched his stomach. Wincing, he stood up to survey the damage. There was a huge, red, sloppy mark down his top — like the kind his Nan left on his forehead whenever she kissed him with her lipstick-covered lips, but bigger.

"Quick! Take it off before it gets any worse!" his dad ordered.

"But I'm not wearing anything under it," Ryan whimpered.

"Tough."

Ryan dutifully removed his hoodie and passed it to his dad, who strode to the little laundry room off the kitchen.

"All I do is washing," muttered his dad.

Ryan rubbed his arms to stay warm. "You can't restrict who follows my account, Mum. That's censorship. It's against my rights."

His mum held his phone aloft. "THIS is not a right! It's a privilege! And until you can appreciate all the privileges you have, it stays with me," she said, as she slid the phone down her top.

She liked putting stuff down her top: her keys, her wallet, half a sausage roll ("to keep it warm"). She said it was the safest place her things could be. However, what made it the safest place HER things could be also made it the WORST place RYAN'S things could be.

He shivered. Not because he was topless, but because his precious phone had been exiled to his mum's sweaty sports bra.

Lily formed a rectangle with her hands and used it to frame Ryan in her sight. "It's a shame I don't have an account, because this would have made an EXCELLENT stream."

Ryan's mum gestured at the squished pizza box. "Lily, empty that into the black compost bin in the backyard and then stick it in the bin with the yellow lid."

"What?! I'M the one who made it — HE'S the one who ruined it! Make HIM do it!" Lily snapped.

Their mum closed her eyes and rubbed her temples. "Please, Lily."

Ryan's sister huffed and took the box off the table, just as his dad plonked a large pot of slimy green slop in its place.

"Good thing I made extra stew."

Ryan smirked at Lily as she pushed past him.

"Mmm, lucky you! Delicious stew!" he whispered.

"You might wanna check all the lumps in your bowl," she said, sneering. "Just in case I find some crickets near the compost bin …"

He shivered again.

"Oh for goodness' sake, Ryan, go put on a top!" his mum hissed.

Exhausted, woeful and cold, Ryan trudged out of the kitchen and up the stairs.

Little did he know, he would not come back down.

CHAPTER 8

Convinced that his sister might still do something to his dinner, Ryan decided to skip it and stay in his room.

He tried to stream from his laptop, but the parental controls his mum had placed on his account made his channel impossible for the public to find. As much as he searched, there didn't seem to be a way to turn them off.

Ryan gave up and decided to watch Grimmf's channel instead, but annoyingly, it seemed to be one of the rare moments when Grimmf wasn't online.

Normally when Ryan wasn't streaming or watching Grimmf, he hung out with Ishaan. But with that option unavailable, the only thing he could do was ... homework.

Ancient Egypt turned out to be surprisingly compelling. Ryan found an online quiz which toldhim which ancient Egyptian god he was (Amun, apparently). And while looking up some websites Ms Strapp had suggested, Ryan discovered that a kid called Ptolemy became a pharaoh when he was the same age as him!

He was in the middle of reading an article about how Ptolemy was poisoned by his older sister, Cleopatra, when Lily appeared in the doorway.

"THINK FAST!" she yelled as something crinkly thwacked him in the face.

"ARGH! LILY!"

"I said, 'THINK FAST'!" she retorted.

"There's a sign on the door for a REASON!" Ryan grunted, as he tried to work out where the mystery object had landed amongst the mess.

"I wasn't sure if the sign was aimed at ME, or a DIFFERENT Lily."

"It's ALWAYS aimed at YOU! Leave me alone! I'm doing my homework!"

Lily ignored his demand and tiptoed over the clutter to his desk.

"Geez, your room's a tip!" she said, kicking at a mound of clothes like it was a pile of autumn leaves.

"CAREFUL!!!" Ryan said, scooping something up from the floor. "You almost kicked my Willy!"

Willy Wormington was Ryan's most treasured childhood toy. It was made from an old sock stuffed with uncooked rice and had buttons for eyes. Ryan cradled it protectively in his arms.

"Don't leave it on the floor then!" his sister scolded. "It should be thrown out, anyway. It's starting to smell like a rancid burrito."

Ryan glared at her. "Is that why you're here? To get revenge by throwing out everything I love?"

"What? No! Trust me, when I get revenge, YOU'LL know it!"

Lily side-stepped a heap of hoodies and bent over to retrieve the item she'd chucked at his face. It was a packet of Grennies — Ryan's favourite snack.

"I'm here 'cause I thought you might be hungry," she said with pity in her eyes.

She was right. Ryan WAS hungry! He snatched the bag of crispy cheese treats from her grasp and tore into it.

"Thank you," he mumbled as he shovelled the tiny grenade-shaped snacks ravenously into his mouth.

The Grennies exploded with delicious intensity whenever he crunched and covered his tongue in bright orange flavouring. Thanks to his lack of dinner (and barely any lunch), they tasted EVEN better than usual!

Lily peered at his laptop. "Oooh! Cleopatra! Did you know she bathed in sour donkey milk?" she said, as if it was gossip.

Ryan DIDN'T know it, but he didn't want Lily to have the satisfaction of KNOWING he didn't know it.

"Yes. I DID know that!" Ryan said through a mouthful of mush.

"You know, ass is another word for donkey. So Ms Strapp can't tell you off if you say that Cleopatra bathed in sour ass milk."

"Nice try, Lily!" Ryan said as he tipped the final crumbs into his gaping gob. "You're just trying to get me in trouble as payback!"

Lily grinned. "You're getting smarter. Guess I'll have to think of something else. I'm off to bed. Don't stay up all night staring at screens, or you'll end up in hospital like that girl."

The girl Lily was referring to had become something of an urban legend in Horror Heights. She'd been found unconscious in front of her computer three years earlier and had been in an unresponsive state ever since. Grown-ups liked to use the story to scare children off their devices, but Ryan knew the truth.

"Ish's mum said it was caused by a brain issue, NOT a screen! And SHE'S a urologist!"

Lily snickered. "Ish's mum is a NEUROLOGIST, not a UROLOGIST, you peanut! A neurologist is a doctor who specialises in BRAINS. A urologist is a doctor who specialises in WEE!"

"Yeah, well, you need BOTH because you have pee for brains!" he shot back.

"Well, at least I'm not a smelly little egg," she said with a wink. As she left, she added, "G'night, Ry! And YOU'RE WELCOME for the Grennies."

Ryan was about to get back to his homework when he heard his sister shriek from the bathroom.

"RYAN!!! WHAT DID YOU DO TO MY TOOTHBRUSH?!?"

CHAPTER 9

It was almost midnight by the time Ryan finished his ancient Egypt poster. He could have stopped earlier and finished it over the weekend, but he'd found it oddly relaxing. Plus, he enjoyed staying up after his family went to bed – it was the second-best thing to having the house to himself.

He put on his headphones and logged into his streaming account just as Grimmf went live. Despite the time, the chat room was abuzz. Grimmf had fans in every time zone, so they streamed around the clock – sometimes even in different languages.

The chainsaw and other items from lunchtime were gone. Instead, Grimmf's studio was back to its immaculate and empty state. Ryan wondered if Grimmf ever had to help clean up, or if their production team did all of it.

He could only imagine what it felt like to be as

famous as Grimmf. To be universally adored and loved. To have a never-ending supply of things to do and play with. To never be bothered by bossy and embarrassing parents, or irritating siblings, or jealous friends. Yet, for some reason, none of Ryan's friends or family seemed to understand WHY he wanted to be a professional streamer!

"Hi, Grimmions! It's me! The one-and-only Grimmf!" said the streamer. "I hope you're having a good ... uh ... What day is it, again?"

The chat room was inundated with replies.

Grimmf laughed, "Most of you are saying 'Friday' so we'll go with that! I hope you're having a great Friday! If not, that's okay — just tell me what you want and hopefully I can cheer you up!"

As the other subscribers flooded the chat room with requests for speedruns, unboxings, and reaction videos, Ryan could only think of ONE thing which would cheer him up after the day he'd had ...

@ryanlols: I want to be Grimmf.

The request drowned in a sea of a thousand other "I wants".

DING!

The hidden gift compartments popped open from the white studio walls. However, instead of investigating their latest haul, Grimmf stared at the camera with an odd look on their perfect, symmetrical face.

"Sorry, Grimmions! Something's just come up!" they stammered. Then the stream froze.

A pop-up appeared on Ryan's screen.

> **Switch User request accepted.** ×

Ryan had no idea what it meant, but pop-ups were rarely a good thing.

NO!!! NOT A VIRUS! NOT NOW! he silently panicked.

He was about to turn his laptop off and on again when ANOTHER pop-up appeared.

> **Please look into the camera on your device.** ×

Ryan relaxed.

It wants to verify my identity. Good. Must be a security update, he thought.

He smiled at the laptop's tiny lens.

The screen flashed brightly – brighter than ANYTHING Ryan had EVER seen.

Then everything stopped.

Not just Ryan's laptop …

EVERYTHING.

CHAPTER 10

Everything (light, sound, objects, direction, gravity, time — all of it) ceased to exist. Everything...

... except for Ryan.

All he could see was never-ending darkness and all he could feel was an overwhelming sensation of weightlessness.

Ryan floated in the sea of nothingness for a few seconds (or possibly hours, or days — there was no way of knowing), until the laws of physics kicked back in, and he started to descend.

Rapidly.

He couldn't describe it as falling — he'd tried enough parkour to know what THAT felt like. It was more like he was being dragged down by something — as if he was a helium balloon, and someone was pulling on the string.

A small white square appeared below him. It wasn't

until it started to grow that Ryan realised it WASN'T a small white square at all — it was just very far away. And at the rate he was sinking, soon it would be a LARGE white square. A LARGE white square with a red Ryan-shaped splat in the middle!

Ryan closed his eyes and braced himself for impact.

But …

Instead of crumpling in a heap, his feet planted themselves firmly on the ground and he jolted to a halt. It was the same sort of jolt he felt whenever his legs decided to wake him up by randomly kicking on their own accord in his sleep.

He tried to open his eyes, but the infinite black had been replaced by a blinding endless white.

With his eyes still closed, Ryan patted himself down to check for injuries. He felt tingly, but unhurt. Then he took a few steps to test his balance. All was going well until he walked into something — which was an odd thing to happen in an unending white void.

Of course, Ryan wasn't IN an unending white void. When he took a step back and let his eyes finally adjust to the light, he found that he was actually facing a white wall.

The wall was covered in a faint pattern of stripes and squiggles and had a red light box mounted to it, which was switched off. The light box said,

NOW LIVESTREAMING

in bold, white lettering. Below the sign was a huge desk with a blank widescreen monitor perched on top of it – which was what Ryan had walked into.

Behind him were three more white walls, but they weren't patterned like the fourth wall. They were smooth, featureless, and totally unmistakable.

They were the walls of a studio.

Not just ANY studio.

GRIMMF'S studio.

CHAPTER 11

Ryan wasn't sure whether to feel excited or terrified. On one hand, he'd always dreamt of being in Grimmf's studio. On the other, he had no idea how he GOT to Grimmf's studio. In the end, he settled for "confused".

"Hello? Grimmf?" Ryan called out nervously.

There was no response.

There was also no door.

At least, not an obvious one. Ryan knew there must be a secret door, but he wasn't sure where. He knocked on one of the smooth white walls to see if it was hollow, but it didn't make a sound.

Duh! It's a soundproof studio! he thought.

While he waited for someone (hopefully Grimmf) to come and explain everything, he took a cheeky peek at Grimmf's set-up.

If he was being honest, it was a bit of a let-down.

Most professional streamers had a separate HD camera, a good quality microphone, streaming deck, and several monitors plugged into a powerful computer. Grimmf didn't have a separate camera, microphone, OR deck. They had ONE monitor, which was plugged into … nothing. Not even a power socket.

Maybe they take all their equipment with them, so it doesn't get stolen, Ryan thought.

The desk was a bit "meh" too. It didn't have any drawers and apart from the monitor, the only items on it were a keyboard and mouse.

Ryan casually picked up the mouse and, to his shock, the monitor lit up. He lifted the screen (which was unexpectedly light considering it was the size of a decent TV) and waved his hand under it to check for invisible wires.

Must use a contact charger built into the desk, he thought.

When he put the screen back down, he realised it was displaying Grimmf's dashboard. It looked like the dashboard for his own account, but with MUCH better stats. According to the channel's insights, thousands and thousands of Grimmf's subscribers were online at that very moment. Grimmf's channel was right at his fingertips!

If Ryan went live, it would be the biggest audience he'd ever streamed to! He could give them his channel's URL and ask them to send a follower request! And if enough of them did it, his mum might give in and deactivate the parental controls!

He cleared his throat. "If it's okay for me to stream, say nothing," he said in a loud voice.

A few seconds passed.

"Guess it's okay then!" said Ryan.

With eager fingers, he clicked "stream preview" to check the quality of the monitor's camera before he went live. To his surprise, Grimmf's face suddenly appeared on the screen.

"G-GRIMMF! Sorry! I – uh – uh—" Ryan tried to explain, just as Grimmf started talking.

They both paused and waited for the other to speak.

Ryan laughed. So did Grimmf.

"You go first!" said Ryan.

Grimmf said the same thing – at the exact same time.

It was then that Ryan noticed something else. His sleeves were different. He looked down at his outfit and gasped. The clothes he'd been wearing in his bedroom had been replaced by an iconic black-and-white tracksuit …

He wasn't talking TO Grimmf …

He WAS Grimmf!

CHAPTER 12

It was all a dream!

It was the only explanation. Unless a mega-rich tech genius had secretly invented a way to insert people into the bodies of their idols and was using it on random kids … but that was a bit of a stretch, even for Ryan. It HAD to be a dream.

No wonder Grimmf's equipment was so underwhelming — it wasn't real!

Well, I guess if I can't be a famous streamer in real life, I might as well be one in my dreams! thought Ryan.

Using the screen as a mirror, he inspected his new, symmetrical features. His eyes sparkled almost as much as his perfectly straight teeth. His cheekbones were so sharp, they made knives jealous. His jawline was so well-defined, it was probably in the dictionary.

Ryan had Grimmf's good looks and Grimmf's studio.

But if he was going to make the most of his dream, he was going to need Grimmf's audience.

He clicked the button to go live.

The "**NOW LIVESTREAMING**" sign above the desk lit up and thousands of viewers immediately poured in. Before he even had time to say hello, they were all clamouring for his attention. It felt good. REALLY good.

"Hey, cheesebutts! Grimmf here! No, not Grimmf. Grimmf! I mean Grimmf!!!"

Ryan shook his head. Every time he said his real name, it came out as "Grimmf".

He spoke slowly. "My name is … Grimmf."

@mA77PaRK3r: We know!

@p0Lly_l9: Did anyone catch their name?

@lynn3M: No, hopefully they'll say it again lol

Ryan gave up. There was no point trying to fight with his own dream.

"Okay, Grimmions, let's do this! What do you want to see me stream about today?"

The chat room flooded with so many requests, they were impossible to read.

DING!

Dozens of trapdoors popped open from the walls on either side of Ryan, revealing a treasure trove of goodies hidden in different-sized compartments.

Just when Ryan thought his dream couldn't get any better, the ENTIRE wall behind him flipped up like a garage door and blended seamlessly into the ceiling. The studio was suddenly TWICE the size as it was before. But that wasn't the best bit ...

Facing him, parked in the newly extended area of the studio, was a sea-green Aston Martin Vulcan!

Ryan punched the air. "YES!!! YES!!! YES!!! THANK YOU!!!"

Ryan ran over to the stunning beast of a machine and sat behind the wheel. The engine revved into life – which startled him – and he exploded in a fit of hysterical giggles. He'd never driven a car before, but he'd played A LOT of racing games. He put his foot on the accelerator …

… and abruptly lurched backwards into the wall.

There was a sickening crunch. His head slammed into the back of the seat so hard, he thought he must have broken his skull. Fortunately, when he got out and checked himself, he seemed completely unharmed.

However, the same couldn't be said for the car. The back of it resembled an accordion.

"Oops," Ryan said, returning to the desk with his head hung in shame.

It was a good thing he was dreaming, because humiliating himself in front of a hundred thousand people in real life would have been worse than the time he called Ms Strapp "Mum" in front of the whole class.

Determined to enjoy his dream as much as possible, he looked around to see what else the subs had requested. He reached into a long, narrow compartment in the wall closest to him and pulled out …

"A CROSSBOW!!!"

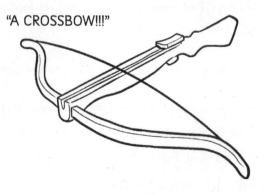

@9EneV1EvE: watch them fire it backwards into themselves by accident

@ScaryBeanEggo: omgosh I can't look!!! (/ ω \ )

@weenanpooieb: brb gettin popcorn.

The weapon was already loaded and ready to fire. Ryan raised it up, took aim, and pulled the trigger.

The mechanism was so powerful, the arrow pierced the windscreen of the car before he'd even let go of the trigger. The arrow was firmly embedded in the centre of the driver's seat headrest. Amazingly, the window remained intact, except for a few cracks around a small arrow-hole.

Ryan dropped the crossbow in astonishment and turned to the monitor. "DID YOU SEE THAT?!"

@b1g_h0ward: CROWBOW HYPE!!!

@ABeeGoalLiar: that was fire

@TumFoodliffe: good luck gettin ur deposit back on that car

Ryan scanned the room for the next thing to play with. A mysterious rectangular black box stood out amongst the colourful toys and shiny gadgets in the other compartments.

He retrieved it from the wall and brought it back to the desk. The chat room was swamped by viewers all wanting to know what it was.

"I dunno ..." said Ryan, giving it a shake. "But it's pretty heavy."

As he shook it, something down the side of the box

glistened. He held it at an angle to get a better look.

"Hang on, it says something!"

The letters were black, like the box, but they glinted when they caught the light. His eyes grew wide as he read the letters aloud ...

"P ... H ... E ... N ... E ..."

The chat room went WILD.

@r0513_j0N3Z: No. Way.

@TurkleGTurkington: \ (°○°)/

@ahmadwhu: faaaake

Ryan was stunned. He'd always wanted to see a Phene up close! Best. Dream. EVER!

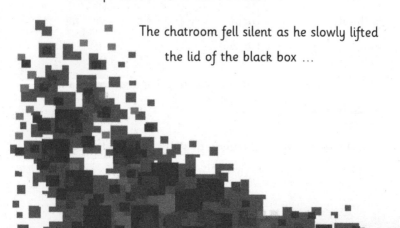

The chatroom fell silent as he slowly lifted the lid of the black box ...

CHAPTER 13

"It's a hammer," Ryan said, crestfallen.

He showed the viewers the contents of the Phene box and a tidal wave of outraged reactions inundated the chat.

> **@A_Hugh_Bert:** y would u do this to us Grimmf???
>
> **@w00denbarnes:** yo you need a refund! You got pwned!
>
> **@ahmadwhu:** told u it was a fake (- ‿ ͡ ृ)

"Even in my DREAMS I can't get my hands on a Phene!" Ryan muttered under his breath.

He peeled off a thin layer of silver plastic which was wrapped around the hammer's handle. It wasn't as satisfying as peeling the plastic off a new phone screen, but it was better than nothing. The discarded wrapping gently drifted down like a feather and landed on the keyboard. Then it lit up.

"WHOA!" said Ryan.

@okdoody: what is it

@SaspotL: WHAT

@dundee_abs21: sksksksk

The handle hadn't been wrapped in plastic! It had been wrapped in a PHONE!

Ryan held the Phene up to the monitor.

@LooEase_G: wut

@LetsEatYummyBurgers: where did that come from??

@somenewHD: did I miss something?

He turned the phone sideways. It was so thin, it seemed to vanish.

"BEHOLD! THE PHENE!"

He scrunched it up, then smoothed it back out into a rigid rectangle again, like magic.

"It really IS the thinnest, lightest, most flexible phone!" he said in awe.

Then Grimmf's classic, charismatic smile crept across his face. The hammer finally made sense.

"Let's see if it's as indestructible as they say!"

He placed the paper-thin phone on the desk and lifted the hammer. With a series of blows, he hit it so hard, it dented the desk. But the phone? It was as impeccable as Dane's report card (and Dane was the best student in his class).

Thanks to Ryan's numerous creative attempts to destroy the Phene (including rolling it up into a little ball, shoving it up his nostril and shooting it out by blowing his nose), Grimmf's channel gained several thousand followers. The adrenalin rush from seeing the numbers rise was like nothing he had ever experienced before.

In his dream, he felt just like the Phene:

indestructible.

CHAPTER 14

Ryan didn't like virtual reality games. They made him motion sick. But the VR headset was the only thing left in the walls' compartments that he hadn't played with, and he knew all too well how important it was to give the subs what they wanted. It was bad enough that he was a failed streamer in real life – he couldn't bear the thought of being a failed streamer in his dreams as well. So, he reluctantly played a horror game Grimmf's fans had chosen. On the plus side, he was too scared to feel sick.

In hindsight, he should have done the VR first, while the studio was clear. The floor was an obstacle course of randomly gifted items, including a tiny clown bike (which he'd managed to ride halfway across the room before falling off), a set of weights (which were far too heavy, even for Grimmf's athletic physique), a silly boardgame (which threw gunk at his face if he got an answer wrong), and a robot sloth (which was either broken,

or had been specifically designed to sing K-Pop and do nothing else). He kept tripping over everything and had set the alarm off on the Aston Martin by bumping into it – twice.

The viewers didn't pay much attention to Ryan's point-of-view-feed of the game. They took way more pleasure in watching the main feed of Ryan stumbling around the studio. Every time he walked into something, he got loads of reactions.

Ryan entered a room in the game. It was empty apart from a creepy, faceless jester doll in the middle of the room.

@Might_T_Hat_On: pick up doll!

"Are you sure?" he asked, hoping he wouldn't have to.

@AntHillY: yesssss do it

@S_MoBaM: get the evil jester doll!

He gulped and anxiously reached down.

As he picked up the doll in the game, he unexpectedly grasped something solid in the studio.

"AAAHHHHH!!!"

Without thinking, he hurled the unknown object at the floor. It started singing a janky version of "Butter" by BTS.

It was the robot sloth.

Ryan had also thrown down the doll in the game. Its head had fallen off, and crawling out of its hollow body were hundreds and hundreds of …

"CRICKETS!!!" Ryan shrieked.

But to his relief, as they scurried closer, he

realised he was wrong.

"Oh, phew! They're just spiders."

@bevan_delved: how are spiders BETTER than crickets?!?

@N0zJOrris: grimmf with crickets = \ (º □ º |||)/
grimmf with spiders = ‾_(ツ)_/‾

@babycakespittle: y don't u like crickets?

Ryan tried to change the subject. "Do you want me to play a different game, or stick with this one?"

It didn't work.

@LiaRinaEnt: Hahaha you screamed so loud when you thought it was crickets! And that was just a game!

@dizzyrayberch: imagine if it WAS crickets and it WASN'T a game

@KT5t0rey: Now I want to see THAT!

A high-pitched tone started to softly ring in Ryan's ears.

He removed the headset. "Is that coming from the game?"

It wasn't. And it was getting louder.

The shrill trill grew so intense, Ryan felt like his head might explode.

Soon, the walls were humming with the unmistakable piercing chirps of ...

"Crickets ..." he whispered.

He had just enough time to hold his breath before –

DING!

CHAPTER 15

THOUSANDS UPON THOUSANDS OF CRICKETS
SPILLED INTO THE STUDIO.

They cascaded from every compartment in the left
wall. They overflowed from every opening in the right
wall. They bounded out of the back wall, bounced over
the Aston Martin, and leapt up Ryan's legs. One even
perched on his shoulder, as if Ryan was a pirate who
couldn't afford a proper parrot.

Even though he was terrified, he kept his mouth
shut and refused to scream. He'd once heard that when
someone dies in their dreams, they die in real life. He
was 99% sure it was a lie, but he couldn't risk dying in
his sleep just because he choked on a cricket during an
imaginary streaming session.

Ryan needed somewhere safe to breathe.
Somewhere with doors. Somewhere like ...

The car!

Tripping over a foot spa (the least exciting item he had been gifted), he stumbled across the studio to the Aston Martin and climbed into the passenger side. He slammed the door behind him – and regretted it instantly.

The force of the slam caused the cracked windscreen to shatter, showering Ryan in tiny shards of glass. And more crickets.

Feeling around for something to fend off the plague of pests, his fingers wrapped around the arrow, which was still stuck in the chair next to him. He would have preferred a can of bug spray, but it was better than using his bare hands.

Ryan plucked the arrow from the driver's seat headrest like he was Arthur removing the sword in the stone. Except Arthur used his weapon to rule a kingdom, while Ryan used his to swat at a swarm of itty-bitty beasties. It had the expected effect: diddlysquat.

Ryan was running out of ideas – and oxygen. He needed to get the crickets away from his mouth so he could take a breath without inhaling one.

He leapt out the car and tried to shake the creepy critters off, but they clung to his clothes like little rodeo riders. The texture of Grimmf's tracksuit was perfect for their grippy feet to grab on to.

That's it! he thought. It's not ME they're attracted to – it's the fabric! All I have to do is take off the tracksuit!

He tugged and yanked at the outfit, but it wouldn't budge. It was as if the material was melded to him – like it was part of his body.

WHAT IS HAPPENING?!

He was covered in crickets, his face was turning purple, and his clothes were somehow also his skin: Ryan's dream had become a NIGHTMARE!

And it was time to wake up.

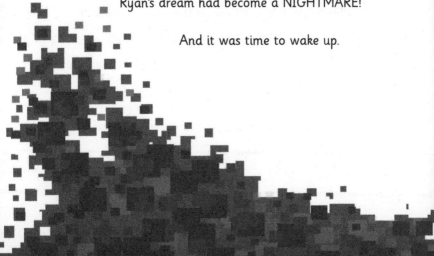

CHAPTER 16

Still holding his breath and surrounded by crickets, Ryan pinched himself.

Nothing happened.

He did it again, harder.

Nothing.

He scrunched his eyes closed and then opened them again.

He was still stuck in his nightmare.

WAKE UP! he shouted inside his head.

He slapped himself across the face a couple of times. Unfortunately, rather than wake himself up, all he managed to do was squish a couple of crickets into his cheeks.

He had no other option than to try his least favourite way of waking up ... Wetting himself.

He scrambled over to the foot spa and shoved his hand in the warm water. Sadly, all it did was make his hand warm and wet.

Why isn't this working?! It worked on Mo!!!

A disturbing notion occurred to him ...

If I can't wake up, then ... I can't be asleep! Which means ... I'm ACTUALLY in Grimmf's body! In Grimmf's studio! With no exit! And thousands of crickets!

He ran back to the desk and frantically searched for the Phene. As impressive as the super-slim, super-light, and super-flexible phone was, it was also SUPER hard to find!

Ryan rifled through the unboxed products and leftover packaging scattered across the desk, like a leaf-blower gone rogue.

As soon as he found the Phene under the keyboard, he called the police.

An error message appeared.

> **Unable to connect: no signal or Wi-Fi found**

Every time he tried, it said the same thing.

His cheeks were turning blue. Ryan couldn't hold his breath for much longer. He looked into the monitor's camera and pleaded with his eyes for the subs to make it stop.

But they didn't. They thought it was hilarious.

@HbrtClnkrdnk: I think I saw Jiminy!

@b0bditt0: jajajajaja Grimmf's lost it!

@FlickWardM8: haven't seen this much cricket since the Ashes!

Ryan's knees buckled and he fell to the white, polished floor.

If Grimmf's subscribers weren't going to help him, he wasn't going to give them the satisfaction of watching him suffer. With the little strength he had left, he lifted his hand up to the desk and hit the "End Stream" button.

The "**NOW LIVESTREAMING**" sign flicked off.

CHAPTER 17

The crickets disappeared.

As did the car, the crossbow, the tiny bike, the weights, the boardgame, the VR headset, the foot spa, and everything else he'd received. The compartments in the walls vanished and the room promptly returned to its original size.

Ryan gasped. Not just from shock, but because he'd been holding his breath for AGES!

Once he recovered, he went to the computer to search for the police. Except he couldn't. There was no navigation bar and he couldn't minimise or close the main window. The keyboard shortcuts had also been disabled. The only thing he could access was the dashboard for Grimmf's account – and it didn't have an option to log out!

Most tech problems Ryan encountered could be fixed by switching something off and on again. But without a computer tower, plugs, or buttons on the monitor, he didn't know HOW to switch it off and on again!

"WHAT'S GOING ON?!?!" Ryan shouted.

The room was silent.

Ryan had never felt more confused and alone. What if no one came to get him? What if he was trapped for ever? What if he never saw his family – or Ishaan? The last thing he'd said to his best friend was, "You've ruined my life. You're dead to me." He hadn't meant it, but without a way to contact him, Ishaan would never know …

Then it hit him – he COULD contact Ishaan!

Ryan jumped back to his feet. "I CAN DO A PSST!" he yelled joyfully.

It wasn't as rude as it sounded. "PSST" was short for "Personally Sent Secure Transmission" and was how online users privately messaged or video called each other on the platform.

Ryan typed Ishaan's username into the dashboard's search box and cheered when @PlentyOfIsh came up as an online account.

I'll be saved in no time!

... he thought.

CHAPTER 18

Ishaan appeared on the screen with his warm, clay-coloured bedroom walls behind him. He reeled in shock when he saw Ryan.

"GRIMMF?! Oh my gosh! It IS you! I mean, I know you have the blue tick, but I just assumed you were a hacker, or scammer, or catfish or something!"

"No, Ish! It's me! Grimmf!" Ryan still couldn't say his own name. "Sorry! Hold on!"

He typed "It's Ryan!" in the private chat box and pressed enter.

> **@GrimmfOfficial:** It's Grimmf!
>
> **@GrimmfOfficial:** *Grimmf

He tried writing his name letter by letter.

> **@GrimmfOfficial:** G
>
> **@GrimmfOfficial:** R

@GrimmfOfficial: I

@GrimmfOfficial: MMF

"ARGH! I can't even tell you in writing!" said Ryan.

Ishaan squinted. "Tell me what?"

"That I'm your brud-for-life!"

"...Ryan?"

"Yes!!!"

Ryan told Ishaan everything that happened after dinner that Friday night.

"I thought it was a dream, but it's not! I don't understand how any of this is possible!" he wailed as he finished explaining.

Ishaan, who had been silent the whole time, exploded. "SERIOUSLY?! Ryan talked you into pranking me?! What a jerk!!!"

Ryan's heart sank. "I swear! This isn't a prank!"

Ishaan was so furious, steam was practically coming

out of his ears. "And YOU'RE a jerk for helping him, Grimmf! You must be desperate for content! Especially if you're trying to convince people that you and Ryan Freaky Friday'd!"

"I'm not! I don't even know what that means!"

"The film! Where they swap bodies!" said Ishaan.

"Honestly, Ish, I don't know WHAT happened! I thought I was dreaming up until ten minutes ago!" Ryan said with desperation in his eyes.

Ishaan folded his arms. "Okay, if YOU'RE Ryan, what's your middle name?"

"David," Ryan answered.

Ishaan grunted. He was still unconvinced. "What about MY middle name?"

"You don't have one," answered Ryan.

"Lucky guess!" said Ishaan. "When did we become friends?"

"Three years ago, when you and your mum moved

to our street and Mum and Dad invited you both over for dinner. I remember, 'cause when we were eating, Lily dropped a pea on her lap, and I said 'Oh no! Lily's pea'd herself!' and you laughed so hard you nearly puked!"

Ryan paused and waited for a reaction, but Ishaan said nothing.

"I think that's the REAL reason I wanted to be a streamer," Ryan continued. "I wanted to make people smile. 'Cause making YOU smile feels amazing – it feels the same as finding ten bucks on the street. So I thought, if I could make, like, a thousand people smile, it would feel the same as finding TEN THOUSAND bucks!"

As Ryan spoke, his conscience started to roll around inside his head. It spiralled to the centre of his mind, gathering guilt like a snowball. Then it picked up every painful pang it passed as it slid down the slope of his throat. By the time it reached his chest, the snowball of shame had turned into an avalanche of regret, which made Ryan shiver as it buried his heart.

"I guess I didn't realise that the reason it feels

amazing when I make YOU smile is 'cause, um, I care about you. Y'know?" Ryan said, awkwardly. "You've always looked out for me and made me feel, like, appreciated and stuff. It means a lot. I shoulda told you that earlier, but I was so obsessed with gaining subs, I think I forgot why I was doing it. So, um, I'm sorry. For everything."

Ishaan didn't respond.

"And I'm not just saying that because I need your help," Ryan added.

Ishaan remained motionless.

"Ish?"

"Hello? Oh! You're back! My screen froze! I missed everything after 'Lily dropped a pea on her lap'. Can you say it again?"

Ryan cringed. It'd been hard enough to say it the first time!

"Uh. I was just saying how, um, you mean a lot to me. And, uh. I'm sorry about that text."

"No, you definitely said more than that," said Ishaan. "Go back to the start. What did you say after 'Lily dropped a pea on her lap'?"

"Oh, uh ..." Ryan was about to answer when he noticed the hint of a grin tugging at the corner of Ishaan's lips. "Hey!!! You just want me to say 'Lily's pea'd herself' again!"

Ishaan burst out laughing.

Ryan's heart fluttered. "So you believe it's me?"

Ishaan nodded.

Ryan let out a relieved sigh. Then he bit his lip.

Even though Ryan had Grimmf's face, Ishaan knew what he was thinking.

Yes, I heard everything you said! Ishaan winked.

Ryan blushed.

Then Ishaan stuck out his tongue. Ryan didn't need words to know what it meant.

I forgive you.

CHAPTER 19

"So I think I know what's going on," said Ishaan. "This IS a prank."

Ryan's heart fell. "I promise I'm not pranking you."

"No, you're not pranking ME. Grimmf's pranking YOU!"

Ryan took a moment to process what Ishaan was suggesting.

"Putting a whoopie cushion on someone's chair is a prank," said Ryan. He gestured at his face and surroundings. "THIS is sorcery!"

"I'm not saying it's a SIMPLE prank," said Ishaan.

"But why ME?"

"Exactly! Why YOU?" said Ishaan. "SOMEONE must have asked Grimmf to do it! Someone who knows you love Grimmf and has a reason to prank you."

Ryan threw his hands up. "Oh great, so just literally EVERY PERSON IN THE WORLD!"

"Not necessarily," said Ishaan. "You obviously got to Grimmf's studio SOMEHOW. Do you remember anything weird on Friday night before this all happened?"

"Nope. Well, Lily was nice to me. THAT was weird. But other than that, nothing."

"Lily was nice to you?"

"Yeah. She brought me a pack of Grennies because I skipped dinner," said Ryan.

"As in, Lily-who-said-she'd-make-you-pay, Lily? Sounds pretty sus to me ..."

As the penny dropped, so did Ryan's jaw. "She pulled a Cleopatra!"

"She put sour donkey milk in her bath?" Ishaan asked, screwing up his nose.

"No, she POISONED me! She must've put something

in the Grennies to make me fall asleep!" said Ryan.

Ishaan leapt out of his chair. "That's it! She must have snuck you out the house and into a van, or private jet, or something, which took you to wherever Grimmf's studio is!"

"That still doesn't explain how I got into Grimmf's body, though," said Ryan.

"I don't think you ARE in Grimmf's body," said Ishaan.

Ryan leaned towards the camera so Ishaan could get a good look at Grimmf's features.

"Then WHOSE face is this?!"

"Yours. It just LOOKS like Grimmf's."

"Huh?"

"Are there any mirrors in there?"

Ryan looked around. "Uh … No. But I can see myself on the screen."

"Correction: you can see GRIMMF'S face on the screen."

"Yeah. Same thing," said Ryan.

"Aw, sweet, innocent Ry-Ry," said Ishaan with a smug grin. "Do you think everyone looks the same in real life as they do on-screen?"

Ryan slapped his forehead. He couldn't believe he'd missed something so obvious.

"It's a filter!"

Ishaan nodded. "I reckon that's why you've been glued into the tracksuit. Lily must've done it so you wouldn't be able to see you were still in your own body."

"Clever girl," said Ryan.

"Are you quoting Jurassic Park?"

"Yeah."

"Nice," said Ishaan.

"What about the crickets and the car and

everything? How did it all appear and disappear?" Ryan asked, getting back on track.

"Well, you already know how I think the walls work in Grimmf's studio. They probably programmed a bunch of bots to ask for specific things in the chat room and then loaded the walls from the other side. As for making it vanish, Grimmf has THOUSANDS of fans – I bet at least one of them is a magician who knows a few tricks."

Ryan considered Ishaan's theory. The possibility that his sister had enlisted the help of his favourite streamer AND a magician to tranquillise him, literally stick him in someone else's clothes, move him to a secret location, and lock him in a room with a tonne of crickets didn't exactly fill Ryan with relief. But at least it was an explanation – which was a lot less scary than NOT having an explanation.

Ishaan's mum's voice broke Ryan's train of thought. "Ishaan! Lunch is ready!"

Ryan was stunned. "Lunch?! What time is it??"

"Just after 1 p.m.," said Ishaan.

"Wow! That went FAST! I haven't even slept! I don't feel tired at—"

Ishaan interjected, "Whoa, whoa, whoa! Back up! You haven't slept since FRIDAY?!"

"Yeah! I can't believe it's already been THIRTEEN HOURS!" Ryan replied.

Ishaan looked troubled. "Uh ... Today isn't Saturday."

"Huh? What day is it?"

SUNDAY

CHAPTER 20

"What do you MEAN it's SUNDAY?!" Ryan yelped.

Ishaan angled his phone's camera at the time and date on his watch.

"I've been awake for 37 HOURS?! That can't be right!" said Ryan.

"Maybe after you ate those Grennies, you were asleep for a really long time?" Ishaan suggested. "I'll go to your place now. Once Lily knows that WE know, she'll HAVE to let you out!"

"ISHAAN! LUNCH!" yelled Ishaan's mum from somewhere offscreen.

"I CAN'T! I'VE GOTTA GO TO RYAN'S!" Ishaan yelled back.

"So I haven't eaten for nearly two days?" Ryan said, astounded. "Shouldn't I be hungry?"

Ishaan propped the phone up on his desk and pulled on some socks. "Might be a side-effect of whatever Lily gave you. On the plus side, at least you won't need the toilet!"

Ryan shuddered at the thought of pooping while wearing a tracksuit he couldn't take off.

"FOOD FIRST!!! DOCTOR'S ORDERS!!!" shouted Ishaan's mum.

"Uh oh. What did you do?" said Ryan. "She only plays the 'doctor' card when she's in a bad mood."

"She's on night shifts at the hospital, so this is like, her bedtime," said Ishaan.

"You better go. You're not much help to me if you're grounded. Eat quick. You can start another PSST when you're done," said Ryan.

"You sure?"

Ryan nodded. "Yeah. And thanks, Ish. I mean it. You're my Indiana Jones."

Ishaan smiled. "And you're my hat."

CHAPTER 21

As Ryan waited for Ishaan to call him back, his eyes fell on the fourth wall behind the desk. It was the only part of Grimmf's studio he hadn't properly investigated.

He squinted at the faint pattern. Something seemed off about it – almost chaotic. The stripes and squiggles didn't repeat in a specific order. Ryan reached over the monitor and ran his hand across it. It felt rough.

"That's strange ..." he said under his breath.

He needed a closer look.

It took all the strength he had to drag the huge desk just a few feet out, so he could slip behind it to examine the wall.

What he discovered sent chills down his spine.

He'd been wrong. The fourth wall wasn't covered in a pattern.

The fourth wall was covered in scratches.

Thousands of scratches.

At first Ryan thought they were claw marks. But on closer inspection, he realised they were tallies. He knew what tallies were because Ms Strapp used them to keep track of things, like the amount of times Dane got a perfect score in a test, or how many times she caught JD trying to cheat off Dane's test.

Alongside each tally etched into the wall was a username. Dozens of them. None of the names looked familiar, except for one …

@TOMATOMIC

Why is Tomato Mic on Grimmf's wall?!

He counted the tally next to Tomato Mic's name in his head.

Five, ten, fifteen, twenty, twenty-five, thirty, thirty … three … Thirty-three? Thirty-three WHAT? Followers?

Points? Sausages???

Ryan tried to find @TOMATOMIC so he could ask them about it in a PSST, but they were offline.

Then he received a video call request.

CHAPTER 22

Ryan was greeted by a chin with crumbs around it.

"I ate as quick as I could!" said the chin.

"I can tell!" said Ryan.

"Oops! Sorry!"

The camera pulled out to reveal Ishaan standing on Ryan's doorstep. He wiped his mouth with the back of his spare hand and then used it to lightly knock on the door.

As they waited for someone to answer, Ryan told Ishaan about the discovery. "Why does Grimmf have a bunch of usernames on their wall?"

Ishaan wasn't listening. He was staring at the door. "What if she's not home?" he asked anxiously.

"It's lunchtime on a Sunday, Ish. She probably just got out of bed!" Ryan said. "That's weird, though, right? Tomato Mic didn't have any subs – so how does Grimmf even know their name?"

Ishaan had already raised his hand to knock again when he looked quizzically at Ryan. "Tomatoes?"

At that exact moment, the door swung open and – to his utter dismay – Ishaan inadvertently knocked on Lily's forehead.

Ryan couldn't tell what happened next, because the feed went blurry, but when it returned, all he could see was Ishaan's face pressed against the carpet in the entranceway.

"Ahhh! It was an accident! Honest! I'm sorry!" Ishaan wailed.

"You're lucky you have such a weak knock!" Lily snarled. She hauled him up to his feet. "Ryan's not here, anyway."

"Oh, we already know THAT!" said Ryan.

Lily glanced at the phone, then looked up at Ishaan with an intrigued look on her face. "Isn't that the streamer Ryan's obsessed with?"

"Don't act like you don't know it's me!" said Ryan.

Lily chortled. "Wow, arrogant much?"

"We know you're pranking Ryan," Ishaan blurted.

"What? I'm not pranking Ryan! Why would I prank Ryan? I don't even know HOW to prank! Who said anything about pranking?" stammered Lily.

She was hiding something, Ryan was sure of it.

"Give her The Stare!" he said.

Ishaan fixed his eyes on hers.

Ryan expected Lily to put up more of a fight, but as soon as Ishaan began his visual lie-detecting test, she crumbled.

"Fine! I AM pranking him!" Lily confessed. "But Ryan started it!"

"Yeah, but Ryan never resorted to ABDUCTION!" Ishaan shot back.

Lily's face fell. "I didn't think of it like that … Now I

feel really mean. I guess I should let the little guy out."

"Ya think?!" yelled Ryan.

Lily trudged up the stairs. Ishaan followed and Ryan was treated to another close-up of his best friend's chin.

"Uh, where are you going?" said the chin.

"To let him go, obvs!"

She must be getting her phone so she can tell Grimmf to release me, thought Ryan.

"Whoa!" said the chin. "This looks nice!"

Ryan couldn't see what Ishaan was looking at, but he could tell from the hint of baby-blue in the background that they were in his room. He heard the doors to his wardrobe slide open.

"Here he is!" said Lily's voice.

"Huh?" said the chin.

Ryan had no idea what was happening. "I can't see!

Switch cameras!" he said.

"I don't think that's a good idea," said the chin.

"Just do it, Ish!!!"

A giant cricket appeared on the screen.

"EEEEEK!" Ryan squealed as he reeled back from the monitor.

The cricket grew smaller as it was moved away from the camera. It flittered about in a jar Lily was holding, trying to escape.

"I don't normally abduct crickets. I just thought it'd be funny to prank Ryan by hiding this little fella in his wardrobe, so he'd hear it chirping all night."

"THAT'S your prank??" said Ishaan.

"Yeah, I told him I was gonna make him pay!" said Lily.

"So, you didn't kidnap Ryan on Friday night? Or glue him into his clothes while he slept and lock him up for two days? Or hire a magician to help with props and illusions?" asked Ishaan.

Lily laughed. "Of course I didn't! For a start, what you've just described is a CRIME, not a prank. Except, maybe, for the magician part. Secondly, Ryan's been home all weekend!"

Ryan and Ishaan yelped in unison, "WHAT?!"

CHAPTER 23

"Yeah," said Lily.

She was completely unaware of how quickly she'd unravelled Ishaan's hoax theory.

"He's been sucking up to Mum and Dad all weekend. That's probably why you haven't seen him."

"That doesn't make any sense …" Ishaan uttered.

"What do you mean?" asked Lily.

Ishaan held his phone up. "Ryan's been stuck like this in Grimmf's studio all weekend!"

Ryan's head started to spin, like the time he went too fast on the roundabout in the park and threw up on his shoes. If he wasn't being pranked, then something even creepier was happening.

Lily narrowed her eyes at Ryan. "You told Ishaan that you're Ryan?"

"Yes! Because I am!"

His sister waved a hand at Ryan dismissively. "Ish, you gotta block this joker. They're messing with you."

"It's really me, Lily! No cap! Test me!" Ryan implored.

Lily put a hand on her hip and smirked. "Okay … Why doesn't Ryan like crickets?"

Ryan tensed his jaw. "You already KNOW why."

"Yes, but do YOU?" Lily asked.

"I don't know why," mumbled Ishaan.

"That's what I mean. If Ryan wouldn't tell his best friend, then he definitely wouldn't tell Grimmf! So, say it. Prove you're not Grimmf," Lily said smugly, confident he was lying.

Ryan sighed. "A couple of months ago, I choked on a cricket."

"That's it?" laughed Ishaan. "Brud, that's nothing! I once choked on a bead!"

Lily eyed Ryan sceptically. "Tell us why."

"I thought it was a jellybean," said Ishaan.

"Not YOU, Ishaan!" Lily hissed.

Ryan winced with embarrassment. "I ... was ... kissing it."

Ishaan blinked. "Sorry, you were WHAT?"

"I heard crickets are good luck in some countries and I thought maybe if I kissed one and made a wish, it would come true," Ryan murmured. His cheeks singed with humiliation.

Ishaan was struggling to keep a straight face. "And did you wish to choke on a cricket? Because it sounds like it came true!"

"No! I wished for more subs, obviously! But just as I was making my wish, Lily snuck up behind me in the backyard and yelled 'WHY ARE YOU KISSING A CRICKET?!?!' right in my ear and it scared me. So I went, 'AHHH!' and the cricket jumped in my mouth and got stuck in my throat. THEN Lily started smacking my back! She said it was first aid, but I reckon she just wanted to hit me."

"Oh no …" said Lily. The colour had drained from her face. "You ARE Ryan!"

"Facts!" said Ryan.

"But that means …" Lily's voice trailed off. She hunched forward, as if a heavy invisible cloak of concern was draped over her shoulders. "You and Grimmf Freaky Friday'd."

"Am I the only one who hasn't seen that movie?!" said Ryan.

"I was talking about the book," said Lily.

"Either way, it's FICTIONAL," said Ishaan. "People can't switch bodies! That's impossible!"

"Impossible is a state of mind – not a fact," said Lily. "I used to be like you, Ish. But when I was your age, I experienced something impossible and it changed everything."

"Ryan put the toilet seat down?" said Ishaan.

"Oi!" said Ryan.

"Something like that," Lily said, chewing on her lower lip. "What was the last thing you said before you became Grimmf?"

"I didn't say anything," said Ryan. "Unless you count online? I wrote 'I want to be Grimmf' in Grimmf's chat room."

Lily clicked her fingers. "There you go! This is some kind of wish-gone-wrong, or curse, or something!"

"You're saying Grimmf and I ACTUALLY swapped bodies?"

"Uh huh. It'd explain why you've been so evasive this weekend. I should've known something was up when you cleaned your room," said Lily.

"I was wondering why everything was so neat!" said Ishaan. He panned his phone around so Ryan could see the meticulously tidy bedroom.

"Where's all my stuff?!?"

"In your drawers!" said Lily.

"What about Willy Wormington???"

"I think it got thrown out. I'm pretty sure the rice had fermented. It was less 'sock' and more 'saké'," said Lily.

"Nooo! Not my poor little Willy!" Ryan cried.

"Maybe don't repeat that," giggled Ishaan. "So how do we reverse the curse, Lily?"

"I don't know. We'll have to find Grimmf and ask them," Lily said as she motioned for Ishaan to follow her downstairs.

She checked her reflection in a mirror next to the front door and then escorted Ishaan out of the house.

"Luckily," Lily said, as she broke into a jog, "I know where they are."

CHAPTER 24

By the time they reached the sports centre next to the school, the final quarter of the big basketball game was about to begin, and the place was heaving.

Ryan and Ishaan's classmate Mike paced furiously back and forth while addressing his team by the court. Spectators slowly refilled the bleachers, carrying snacks and drinks they'd bought during the break. Ryan's mum was mopping up a spill.

Her face lit up. "Ishaan! Lily! Have you come to help?"

"We can't, Mum! Ryan's stuck and we need to save him!" said Lily.

"Okay, but can you wait until the tournament's finished?" Ryan's mum responded.

"We don't mean stuck HERE!" said Ishaan. He held out his phone.

"It's me!" Ryan said, waving his hands at the camera.

"Oh hello, Grimmf! Is this one of those 'cameo' things? Did Ishaan and Lily pay you to surprise Ryan with a video call? That's a wonderful idea! He's earned it – he's been SO helpful this weekend!" His mum beamed.

Ryan felt like all the air had been sucked out of him.

"MUM, you're not listening to me!" Lily groaned.

"Excuse me, Lily. Don't take that tone with me! You can grab a mop if you want to chat. Otherwise, you can find Ryan in my office. He's printing out some 'NO DRINKS PAST THIS POINT' signs." Then Ryan's mum blew a whistle around her neck loud enough to make all the dogs in the country bark. She stormed off in the direction of some loose children on the court. "OI! DON'T RUN! THE FLOOR'S WET!"

"That's fine. We don't need her help. We just need Grimmf," Lily said.

She led them through some double doors with a

"STAFF ONLY" sign, and up three flights of stairs.

"Mum looked so happy," Ryan said, dejected. "Do you think she likes Grimmf-me more? Does Dad feel the same?"

"They like the help, but they've been too busy to spend any time with you this weekend. They don't like Grimmf-you more," Lily assured him

They turned down a corridor.

"What about you?" Ryan said in a small voice.

"Ry, I wouldn't be HERE if I liked Grimmf-you more. To be honest, you were giving me the creeps. You were so quiet and respectful – it was so boring. I'm GLAD it wasn't you!" said Lily.

Ryan gave a weak, but appreciative smile.

"I didn't get to meet Grimmf-you, but I already know I like you more," Ishaan added.

Lily pointed at an office at the end of the hallway with light seeping out from under the door.

"Well, you'll get to meet Grimmf-Ryan now," said Lily. "That's Mum's office."

CHAPTER 25

The offices they passed as they marched down the hall were eerily quiet. The sports centre staff who usually filled them were all out running the events. The silence, combined with the flickering fluorescent lights running along the ceiling, made the ordinary corridor unusually spooky.

But it was nowhere NEAR as spooky as the feeling Ryan experienced when he saw himself standing in the middle of his mum's office. His tucked-in shirt and recently washed trousers made his body look funny. Like a dog wearing a tuxedo.

Lily raced in and tackled Grimmf-Ryan to the ground. She lay across their back so they couldn't move.

"What are you?" growled Lily.

"Ow!" Grimmf-Ryan moaned into the scratchy, blue carpet.

"What. Are. You?"

"Get off me!"

"WHAT ARE YOU?!"

"What am I supposed to say to that?!"

"I'M A SMELLY LITTLE EGG!!!" Ryan cried.

Grimmf-Ryan tried to turn their head. "Who said that?"

"My baby brother!" announced Lily.

"My brud-for-life!" added Ishaan.

"…Ryan?" Grimmf-Ryan said, astonished.

"The one and only!" said Ryan.

Lily leant down and whispered menacingly in Grimmf-Ryan's ear. "It's over."

"I want to swap back!" Ryan declared.

"But I thought you WANTED to be Grimmf? You were having so much fun!" Grimmf-Ryan wheezed under Lily's weight.

"It STOPPED being fun PRETTY FAST," Ryan said.

"I'm sorry, Ryan. You can't swap back. You can only swap forward," said Grimmf-Ryan.

"What's THAT supposed to mean??" Lily snarled.

Grimmf-Ryan squirmed. "It means, if someone doesn't want to be Grimmf any more, they have to swap with someone else."

Lily glared at them. "Why should we believe a word you say, Grimmf?"

"Because I'm NOT Grimmf! I'm Tom!"

CHAPTER 26

Lily hoisted Tom to his feet by his shirt and pinned him against a filing cabinet. "Who?!"

"Please don't hurt me!" Tom begged. "I'm just a kid, like Ryan! I was in Grimmf's body when Ryan swapped!"

"Why were YOU in Grimmf's body?!" Ryan demanded to know.

"It was an experiment," said Tom. "I was comparing how different streamers communicate with their audiences and I noticed that Grimmf's interests, skills, or language changed whenever someone in the chat room had said, 'I want to be Grimmf'. I wasn't sure if it was linked or just a coincidence, so I tried it. Next thing I knew, I WAS Grimmf!"

"Whatever, TOM, I didn't ask for your life story!" said Lily. She swung him around and shoved him in front of her mum's computer. "Just say it again so you two can swap back!"

"It won't work. I've tried," said Tom as he gazed down at the desk, glumly.

"Prove it," said Ryan.

Tom sighed. "What's your password?"

Ryan tried to whisper it so his sister and his best friend couldn't hear.

"Sorry, I didn't catch that," said Tom.

Ryan's cheeks began to glow. "I-5-H-A-A-N-=-B-R-U-D-4-L-Y-F"

"Aww, your password is 'Ishaan equals brud for life'! That's so cute!" squealed Lily.

Ishaan blushed. "I thought it woulda been 'Grimmion' or 'stream stan' or something like that."

Ryan shifted awkwardly. "Yeah, well, I wanted to make it something easy to remember."

Ishaan beamed.

"Actually, it's safer to change your passwords

regularly," said Tom, ruining the tenderness of the moment. He dramatically pressed Enter. "Aaand, I'm in!"

"Good. Now say you want to be Grimmf," said Lily.

"I can't type in the chat room unless Ryan's streaming," said Tom.

Ryan gulped. "But I'll be bombarded by crickets!"

"Oh no! They might kiss you to death!" teased Ishaan.

"And THAT'S why I didn't want you to know about that!" said Ryan.

Ishaan winked. "If you do this, I promise I will never, EVER mention it again."

It was the last thing Ryan wanted to do, but if it meant getting his body back — and Ishaan's word not to talk about the cricket incident — it was worth it. He closed the PSST and started a stream.

The "**NOW LIVESTREAMING**" sign lit up and thousands of subs populated the chat room.

"Hey, I'm back, what do you want?" said Ryan, unenthusiastically.

@roofishowhard: what's with Grimmf's attitude

@indygillymac: whoa some1's grumpy!

@crispyknight: I want to see crickets! I missed them earlier!

@MareeeeenaK: yeah crickets!

@hbtw36: CRICKET HYPE!!!

Amongst all the requests for crickets, Ryan managed to catch one comment …

@ryanlols: I want to be Grimmf

DING!

A pop-up appeared as the ominous hum of crickets approached.

Switch User requested by @ryanlols.
Accept/Decline
×

Ryan clicked "Accept".

CHAPTER 27

BONG!

> **ERROR: Switch User request denied –**
> **user has already switched.** ×

Multiple trapdoors in the walls and ceiling flew open. Just as the crickets descended, Ryan ended the stream and they disappeared. The light in the red "**NOW LIVESTREAMING**" sign flickered off once again.

Ryan searched for @PlentyOfIsh so he could video call him, but Ishaan's account was offline. His heart raced.

What if Tom's done something to Ishaan and Lily???

As his thoughts started to spiral, he received a video call request from … himself: @ryanlols.

When he accepted it, Ishaan and Lily were hunched over Tom, who was still sitting at Ryan's mum's desk.

"Sorry, you took longer than I expected, and my battery ran out!" said Ishaan.

"I should have said, when you stream, one minute for you is like, ten minutes for us," said Tom.

"Did you get an error message too?" Lily asked shakily.

Ryan nodded. His eyebrows met in worry, then raised like a drawbridge allowing passage to a nose-shaped boat.

"NOW do you believe me?" said Tom. "There's no swap-backs. If there were, I would've swapped back into my own body WEEKS ago."

"So Grimmf's in YOUR body?" asked Ishaan.

"No," said Tom. "Nikki is."

"Who's Nikki?!" said Ryan.

"She's the nineteen-year-old makeup artist who was in Grimmf's body when I said I wanted to be Grimmf," said Tom.

Ishaan tilted his head to the side. "So Grimmf's in NIKKI'S body?"

"Grimmf isn't anywhere!" said Tom. "Grimmf isn't a person …

… it's a bot."

CHAPTER 28

Ish slammed his hand down next to the keyboard. "Stop messing around with us!!!" he fumed.

"It's okay. Let him talk." Ryan folded his arms and leant back. "I want to know why Tom thinks Grimmf is a bot."

"What's a bot?" asked Lily.

"It's a fake account programmed to follow a set of commands," Tom answered. "There's millions of them. Maybe even BILLIONS. Some of them help moderate chat rooms, some remind people to tip the streamer, but most of them are created to follow the people who buy them."

"Why would someone want to buy fake followers?" Lily asked.

"The more followers you have, the more gifts, sponsors, and ad revenue you get," said Ryan.

"Okay, sure. What's that got to do with Grimmf being a bot?" said Lily.

"Well, imagine if, instead of thousands of bots following a real account – thousands of real accounts followed a bot! A bot so advanced that it wasn't just an account, but a whole channel with an interactive environment where subscribers could use the command 'I want' in the chat room to generate 3D renderings of products instantly in-stream!"

Lily sailed her hand over her head. "WHOOSH!"

"Yeah, I'm lost too," said Ishaan.

"He's talking about how Grimmf's studio can magically produce whatever their subs ask for," said Ryan.

"Correct," said Tom. "Think about it. A bot which looked like a flawless human. A bot which could stream non-stop, without the need to sleep, eat, or poop. A bot with access to unlimited resources!"

Ryan gasped. "The perfect streamer!"

"ALMOST perfect!" said Tom, holding up a finger. "It doesn't matter how flawless a streamer looks, or the amount of time and resources they have, they still need ONE thing to set them apart from everyone else."

"One of those silly hats with a propellor on top?" said Lily, sarcastically.

"A personality!" said Tom.

"So Grimmf was designed to take someone else's?" Ishaan shook his head. "I don't buy it. Why didn't Grimmf's programmer just create a personality and write it into the code?"

"If you were colouring in a picture and needed a red crayon, you wouldn't MAKE a red crayon. You'd use one which already existed," said Tom. "Same with Grimmf — there's no point trying to MAKE a personality when there's already fully developed ones out there."

Lily furrowed her brow. "That doesn't explain why Grimmf keeps swapping personalities, though."

"Yes it does," said Tom. "If you wanted your picture

to look interesting, you wouldn't ONLY use red crayon, would you? You'd switch it up! You'd use yellow, or purple, or aquamarine!"

"... And once you're done with the red crayon, you don't need it again. That's why the system won't let us swap back," Ryan added.

"BINGO!" said Tom. "So Grimmf keeps getting passed from one to another — like Creeper."

"Who's Creeper?" Ishaan asked tentatively.

Tom's eyes lit up. "It was the first ever computer virus! It's actually really interesting — I once did a project about it in computer science. If another system on the network was available to infect, Creeper transferred itself and left a message which said, 'I'M THE CREEPER; CATCH ME IF YOU CAN!' Likewise, if another person in Grimmf's chat room is available to infect, Grimmf downloads that person's personality and leaves the other one in their body."

"But how is a computer virus able to infect a human?" said Lily.

"When someone says, 'I want to be Grimmf', it initiates a 'Switch User' sequence, which directs them to look into their device's camera so their personality can be captured," said Tom.

"Yeah, but how can a camera capture someone's personality?" Lily pressed.

"I don't know, I'm only twelve!" Tom exclaimed.

"If I knew I was making myself available to infect when I said, 'I want to be Grimmf', I wouldn't have said it — it was just a random online comment! I didn't think it'd have serious consequences!" Ryan cried.

"Don't beat yourself up," said Tom. "Since Grimmf's channel appeared three years ago, at least a hundred others have made the same mistake."

"How do you know?" Ryan asked.

"The username of every person who's been Grimmf is on the wall behind Grimmf's desk," said Tom. "It's the only part of the room which doesn't reset, so it's the only way to keep track of how many days you've been trapped for. Every now and then I'd have to ask the subs what day it was so I could update my tally. Like I said — time flies when you stream."

"How many days were YOU trapped for?" asked Ishaan.

With the mystery of the fourth wall revealed, a shocking revelation occurred to Ryan.

"Thirty-three …" he uttered.

"That's right," said Tom, surprised.

"You didn't stop watching my streams because I went camping — you stopped watching because you'd become Grimmf!" Ryan stated.

He felt silly for not working it out earlier when he found the usernames on the wall …

"YOU'RE Tomato Mic!!!"

CHAPTER 29

Tom threw his head back and laughed.

"It's pronounced Tom Atomic! But yeah, that's my handle! I didn't think you'd remember me!"

Lily was stunned. "You two know each other?"

"Not personally," said Ryan. "He used to watch my streams, but I hadn't seen him for thirty-three days. I only just made the connection with the tally on the wall."

"When I was comparing how different streamers communicate with their audiences, Ryan was one of them," said Tom. "I couldn't believe my luck when I got the 'Switch User' request from him. I knew from his streams that he had a good family, caring friends and a nice house."

"But what if Ryan's not as lucky? What if a middle-aged sky-diving instructor called Svetlana wants to swap with him?" said Ishaan.

"I can't sky-dive!!!" spluttered Ryan.

"Everyone can sky-dive. Just not everyone knows how to use a parachute," Lily said, matter-of-factly.

"Ryan can decline a 'Switch User' request. Although, it depends how desperate he gets. Nikki was so keen to escape, she accepted the first 'Switch User' request which came in," said Tom. "It helps if Ryan makes Grimmf's life look as desirable as possible. The more fun and subscribers Grimmf has, the higher the chances are that a suitable candidate will want to swap."

Ryan crossed his arms defiantly. "I don't want to swap with a suitable candidate. I want to swap with you."

"I know, but you can't. I reached out to every account listed on Grimmf's wall. Everyone I spoke to said swapping back wasn't an option. And all the other accounts have been deleted or abandoned." Tom's voice began to go up in pitch as he grew more vexed. "I tried to use the 'I want' command to say I wanted to be back in my own body. I tried to leave through the compartments in the walls, I tried deactivating Grimmf's account, I tried hacking the program to rewrite the code — Nikki even tried to create a new account to trick the system! None of it worked!"

"What if Ryan gets a flamethrower and burns down the studio in a blaze of glory?" Ishaan said with a look in his eyes which Ryan found unsettling.

"Nope! You can't destroy anything in the room — including you and the room itself!" Tom said, close to tears. "I've tried every genius idea or clever loophole I can think of!"

"I think it's time to go to the police," said Lily.

Tom put his hand on his chest, insulted. "You think we didn't think of that?! As soon as we realised we couldn't swap back, Nikki told the police everything. And you know what happened?"

"They said they'd get their best team on it and then made you both honorary detectives?" Ishaan said optimistically.

"They told my parents that I was making false reports and wasting valuable police time. Then my parents sent Nikki to live with my grandparents in a town with NO internet and NO reception. They said my obsession with computers had 'warped my mind' and I needed a digital detox. Now I can't even ask Nikki how my family is! I want my own body back so much, but it's im – im – impossible!" Tom folded into a sobbing heap at the desk.

Ryan cleared his throat. "Yeah, well, someone very wise and annoying once told me that 'impossible' is a state of mind – not a fact."

CHAPTER 30

Tom dug his hand into his pocket and produced a lilac handkerchief which Ryan had forgotten he owned. Tom proceeded to dab his teary eyes in a move so classy it made Ryan wonder if he should start using a handkerchief.

"We need to find whoever created Grimmf. And if they won't fix this, I'LL fix THEM!" Lily said, pounding her fist into her palm.

"Easy there, Cobra Kai," Tom said with a sniff. "Even if we COULD find them, we should stay as far away as possible. Grimmf's programmer might not be getting fame, fun, or freebies out of this, but they're definitely getting the Fourth F."

"... Friends?" Ryan asked, looking at Ishaan.

Tom shook his head.

"FIST!" said Lily.

"Fortune!" said Tom. "Any sponsorship money or ad revenue Grimmf makes must be going somewhere! You think they'll help you out if you show up to their home in your karate gear? They've been hacking kids' brains for their own financial gain for three years! They wouldn't think twice about using whatever powerful tech they have to conveniently get rid of you!"

"What about Patient Zero?" asked Ishaan. "The first person who had their brain hacked by the virus might have the info we need to fix the program ourselves."

"No one knows who it is. If they're on the wall, then their account's been closed, because I never found them." Tom paused to flip the handkerchief over and noisily blow his nose while somehow remaining stylish. "I told you before! I've tried every genius idea and clever loophole I can think of!"

"Maybe that's the problem ..." said Ryan. "You're too smart."

Tom chuckled tearily. "Thank you."

"No, I mean it. I think we're missing something

really simple," Ryan said. "We need to stop thinking so much and focus on what's in front of us."

So you DO listen to me? said Ishaan's glistening eyes.

Not as much as I should, Ryan slowly blinked in response.

Tom held his handkerchief up by the corner. It was soaked with schnoz-slime. "You want me to focus on THIS?"

Lily recoiled. "Ew! Put that soggy snot-rag away!"

"It's too wet for my pocket," Tom whined.

"Then throw it in the bin! It's unhygienic!" Lily squealed.

Ishaan leapt to his feet. "QUARANTINE!"

The others stared at him, startled.

"That's how you stop a virus!" said Ishaan.

"Is that a suggestion, or just general health advice?" asked Ryan.

Lily got excited. "He's right! We've been thinking about Grimmf as a computer virus instead of a biological one! Remember when you had that nasty cold, and everyone in the house got sick, even though you never left your room?"

"Yeah, that blowed. Literally," said Ryan.

"It did. But what if, instead, the rest of us had left the house as soon as you got sick," said Lily. "You would've had the whole house to yourself while you got better, and none of us would have been infected. This is the same situation! Grimmf is a nasty cold! We need to clear out the house so you can get better without infecting anyone!"

"What're you saying?" Ryan asked.

"I'm saying …" Lily paused for dramatic effect. "… We have to get rid of your subs."

CHAPTER 31

"I stand corrected," said Tom, impressed. "To my knowledge, no one has ever tried to get Grimmf's subscribers down to zero. It feels counter-intuitive to actively LOSE followers. But it's worth a shot – as long as you're willing to grow your audience from scratch if it doesn't work."

The thought of having to build a following from nothing AGAIN made Ryan feel sick. But not as sick as the thought of accepting his fate.

"I'll do it," he said.

"It's gonna work, Ry! Hang in there!" said Lily.

"My man!" hollered Ishaan.

"It won't be easy. Grimmf has hundreds of thousands of subs," said Tom. He rubbed his chin in a way that made Ryan's face appear far more intellectual than Ryan ever managed to make it look. "Even if you refused to stream, it'd probably take at least a year to lose them all — if not more. Grimmf's account won't let you block anyone, either."

"Hey. If anyone knows how to lose subs, it's THIS guy!" Ryan said, gesturing at himself with his thumbs. "All I have to do is NOT give the subs what they want, and I'll be back in my body in time for dinner. See you on the other side!"

He ended the video call and started a stream.

The "**NOW LIVESTREAMING**" sign lit up.

"Hey, cheesebutts! What do you want?" said Ryan.

The subs proceeded to fill the chat room with requests for the one thing Ryan hoped they'd forgotten about: crickets. Again.

DING!

It wasn't long before the whole room was teeming with bouncing bugs. The subs WANTED to see Grimmf panic. But THIS time, Ryan wasn't going to give the subs what they wanted. Instead, he closed his eyes and did his best to ignore the plague of pests.

After a while, the swarm of insects settled, and their hysterical hum harmonised to become a smooth, soothing song. Ryan opened his eyes to see that the creatures had ceased leaping and his feet were surrounded by a carpet of calm crickets (except for one which was perched on Ryan's shoulder again, like a tiny parrot).

The lack of action disappointed some of Grimmf's subscribers.

@H4rryM1ll3r: dull. I'm out

@RolyPolyGrandma: might resub to Ninja's channel. at least they DO stuff

@M4g1cM1k3: BORING! Bye felicia!

Deprived of the cricket chaos they wanted, a few thousand subs grew disinterested and unsubscribed.

Then Ryan noticed something strange — the crickets had also started to leave! They serenely scurried in succession towards the compartments they'd come out of.

Ryan nudged the one on his shoulder. It seemed less scary than it was before. "Off you go, little buddy!" he said.

It dutifully hopped down his arm and followed the rest of the critters out. As soon as all the crickets were gone, the compartments in the walls snapped shut.

A new batch of requests immediately came in from the many remaining subs.

DING!

The compartments reopened. There was a drone, a popcorn machine, a glittery eye-shadow palette, a cinema-grade projector, a full suit of armour – and a whole bunch of other stuff.

Ryan ignored the treasure trove of goodies around him and tried to think of the most boring topic he could talk about.

"I hear soap scum is hard to clean. Which is ironic because soap is what you use to clean other stuff."

His refusal to engage with his fans and environment worked.

The compartments snapped closed one by one, as another thousand or so followers unsubscribed out of frustration, boredom and spite.

Refusing to react to the requests was relatively easy. Ryan barely blinked when one subscriber requested slime and he was unexpectedly gunged from a trapdoor in the ceiling. But later, he received a request which even a statue would struggle to ignore …

@GJI150816: I want to see PUPPIES

DING!

CHAPTER 32

Two doors popped out of the walls either side of Ryan and twenty of the CUTEST, most roly-poly puppies he had EVER SEEN bounded enthusiastically towards his feet. They pawed at his legs, begging him to pick them up and play with them. They tumbled about and wagged their tails and yapped adorably.

It took every fibre of Ryan's being not to lie on the floor and let them climb all over him.

When the puppies began to whine and howl from the lack of attention, the tone of the chat changed from disappointment to dismay.

@GJI150816: WHY RN'T U PLAYIG WITH THEM??!?

The puppies hung their heads and whimpered as they slowly left.

As torturous as the experience was for Ryan, it paid off. The subscriber count plummeted and dropped even more as word of Grimmf's unwilling behaviour spread to the offline fans.

By the time the dogs had disappeared, and the compartment doors slammed shut, Ryan had less than a thousand followers. Some of them were holding on out of fierce loyalty. Others seemed curious. The rest were worried for Grimmf's wellbeing.

@LokiCambill: u k hun?

@N4tLurpak: I think Grimmf's been working too hard

@KTWillKings: maybe u should take a break?

Ryan didn't want anyone to pity Grimmf, or they might refuse to unsubscribe out of kindness. But he also didn't want them to feel bad for caring.

"Maybe we should ALL take a break?" he said, thoughtfully. "Why watch ME do NOTHING when you could hang out with your friends, or make something, or do your homework?"

@G00dm4nz: Grimmf sounds like my mum

@J_S_120322: life coach doesn't suit you. Go back to gaming

@m0yzeez: homework? I'm an accountant

"Obviously those are just suggestions," Ryan said quickly. "You can do whatever you want."

@HayB00ya: I did but I got arrested jk jk jk!

@stoofnerdherder: I want to unsub to this nonsense lol laterz

@m0yzeez: ugh you're right, I should be at my kid's dance recital right now

The viewers took Grimmf's advice (or lost interest), and the number of subscribers dwindled until there were only two accounts left in the chat room.

@PlentyOfIsh: You did it, brud!

"You watched the whole stream?" said Ryan.

@ryanlols: Yep! We stayed up all night!

It had been mid-afternoon when Ryan had last spoken to Ishaan, Lily and Tom.

"Uh oh … What time is it?" he asked.

@ryanlols: 6am

MONDAY

@ryanlols: Tom says: "I told you time flies when you stream!"

"No kidding!" laughed Ryan. "You're not still at the Sports Centre are you??"

@ryanlols: Hahaha, no. We're at home. Tom and I are on your laptop.

@PlentyOfIsh: I'm in my room.

"Well, I guess we shouldn't waste any more time! I'll do a countdown and you can both unsubscribe. Ready?"

@PlentyOfIsh: Ready!

@ryanlols: Ready.

Ryan couldn't wait to have his life back.

"Five …"

He missed his body, and his tiny bedroom.

"Four ..."

And he missed his brud-for-life and his family.

"Three ..."

He even missed his dad's cooking.

"Two ..."

And he promised never to take any of it for granted again.

"One ..."

@PlentyOfIsh and @ryanlols unsubscribed.

CHAPTER 34

Nothing happened.

Ryan waited.

And waited.

And waited. Until two accounts subscribed to Grimmf's channel.

@ryanlols: What happened?

"… Nothing," said Ryan. His hopes dissolved faster than one of Lily's fancy bathbombs. "The quarantine didn't work. Tom's right. I can't swap back."

@ryanlols: That doesn't mean it didn't work. When you're sick, you don't get better as soon as you quarantine. You need time and medicine.

@PlentyOfIsh: Don't give up! I'm gonna speak to a neurologist about your situation!

"How would a pee doctor help?" Ryan asked tearfully.

@PlentyOfIsh: ?

@ryanlols: Ry's thinking of a urologist

"Oh yeah. I keep getting those two confused."

@PlentyOfIsh: I meant my mum! She just got home from her night shift!

@ryanlols: Nice thinking, Ish!

Ishaan disappeared from the chat room.

"Lily." Ryan sniffed.

@ryanlols: Yeah?

"What if Ish's mum can't help me?"

@ryanlols: Then we'll come up with another plan.

"I don't wanna be stuck like this for ever," said Ryan. A lump started to form in the back of his throat.

@ryanlols: You won't, mate. I promise.
@ryanlols: hey ryan tom here. is there anyone u know who might want to swap? someone at school or something so it wouldn't b that different?

Ryan shook his head. "I don't want to swap with anyone."

@ryanlols: i know but u might have to

Ishaan re-entered the chat room.

@PlentyOfIsh: Back!
@PlentyOfIsh: I told her everything.

"What did she say?"

@PlentyOfIsh: She said it was a very imaginative story, but it is scientifically impossible.
@PlentyOfIsh: Then I said impossible is a state of mind and she told me to go back to bed
@PlentyOfIsh: Sorry Ry. I'll ask her again, later, when she's had her coffee.

"Lily!" Ryan wailed. He needed his big sister to tell him everything was going to be okay.

@ryanlols: she just went to her room

Ryan slumped over and sobbed into the keyboard.

@ryanlols: can i do anything to help?

Ryan lifted his head and wiped his nose on the sleeve of Grimmf's tracksuit. "Yeah. Can you please apologise to Mo and Yas and everyone else I pranked at school?"

@ryanlols: absolutely

"And don't tell Ms Strapp that Cleopatra bathed in sour 'ass' milk. Even if Lily says you should."

At that moment, Grimmf gained a third subscriber and a new user entered the chat room.

@KarateLily13: Hey! It's me!

"Lily? Did you create an account?" Ryan asked as the lump in his throat tightened.

@KarateLily13: Yeah. I wanted to be KarateLily, but the first 12 were taken.

"Why?"

@KarateLily13: I guess I'm not the only Lily who does karate?

"No, I mean why did you create an account??"

@KarateLily13: I had to, for my other plan.

@KarateLily13: I want to be Grimmf.

DING!

CHAPTER 35

Switch User requested by @KarateLily13.
Accept/Decline
×

Ryan stared at the pop-up.

"What're you doing?" he croaked.

@KarateLily13: Keeping my promise.
@KarateLily13: I won't let you stay stuck as Grimmf
forever.

"But then YOU would be stuck as Grimmf for ever,"
Ryan whispered.

@KarateLily13: Maybe.
@KarateLily13: Maybe not.
@KarateLily13: Don't worry about me, I'll work
something out.

"Why would you do this for me? I've been such a
bad brother ..."

> **@KarateLily13:** It's not like I'm the perfect sister.
> **@KarateLily13:** I bullied you A LOT when we were younger.
> **@KarateLily13:** Let me make it up to you.

"No, I can't. But thank you," said Ryan. The lump in his throat was so tight he was barely audible.

> **@ryanlols:** i think u should take it
>
> **@PlentyOfIsh:** me too

Ryan shook his head. "I don't want to be Lily."

He clicked "Decline".

> **@KarateLily13:** Ryan!
> **@KarateLily13:** I know it's not your body, but you would've had the same parents and the same house!
>
> **@PlentyOfIsh:** and we'd still live on the same street!

"But I want Lily to stay Lily and ..." Ryan's voice faded before he could finish his sentence. He typed into the chat box.

> **@GrimmfOfficial:** I want to be myself.

DING!

Without warning, the floor swung out from beneath Ryan's feet like a giant trapdoor and dropped him into the infinite void of nothingness.

The end ...

... thought Ryan, as a luminous square of white above him got smaller ...

and smaller.

It was the only way he was able to tell he was falling.

This is it, he thought. I broke the program and now I'm going to be stuck in oblivion for the rest of eternity!

CHAPTER 36

Despite the prospect of spending an infinite amount of time in an infinite black abyss, Ryan didn't regret turning down Lily's "Switch User" request. If anything, it made him feel better about his impending doom.

As the white square above him shrank out of existence and he pondered his fate, a new square appeared below him.

A baby-blue square.

The faster he fell, the bigger the square got, until he was sure he was about to pass straight through it.

He closed his eyes, and the sound of rushing wind filled his head, like he was being sucked into a vacuum cleaner. Suddenly, his body was caught by something firm. The sound stopped and all he could hear was the heavy rhythm of his own heart pounding.

It felt as if he'd been holding his breath for hours

and he gasped as air forced its way into his lungs.

Over the top of his heartbeat, he heard a familiar, muffled voice.

"Hello??? Are you okay???"

Ryan opened his eyes and tried to stand up, but everything was out of focus and his legs wouldn't move. A blurry shape hovered directly in front of his face.

"Can you hear me???" said the shape.

Ryan nodded.

"Good. And what are you?"

There was a dull ache in Ryan's thighs.

"Why do my legs hurt?" he whispered.

"Just answer the question," said the shape. "What are you?"

As Ryan's sight returned, the blurry shape and the source of the pain became clear.

It was Lily. She was sitting on his lap.

"What are you?" she repeated.

He was too tired and weak to laugh, but he was able to summon a smirk.

"I'm a smelly little egg," he croaked.

Lily blinked back tears as she smiled.

"And WHO are you?"

"… Ryan."

Relief overwhelmed him.

He could say his name.

CHAPTER 37

Ryan and Lily's moment of triumph was interrupted by a knock on the front door.

"Ish! You're here early! Are you joining us for breakfast?" Ryan heard his dad ask.

There was no answer. Just the sound of Ishaan racing up the stairs.

"Guess you're not a morning person," chuckled Ryan's dad as he returned to the kitchen.

Ishaan burst into Ryan's room, wide-eyed and breathless.

Without saying a word, he marched over to Ryan, grabbed him by the shoulders and gave him The Stare. Within seconds, Ishaan's face was invaded by a smile so big, his eyes were overtaken by his cheeks.

"It's YOU!!!" he cheered, shaking Ryan with joy.

"Ye-e-e-p it's me-e-e," Ryan warbled as Ishaan rocked him back and forth.

"Guys! Look!" said Lily.

She pointed at a notification on Ryan's laptop.

@GrimmfOfficial is now livestreaming.

Grimmf's blank channel whirred into life and the streamer appeared on the screen.

"Ryan! Lily! Ish! Are you there?! It's me, Grimmf — ugh, you know who I mean!"

Ryan joined the chat room.

@ryanlols: Tom?

"The one and only! Is that YOU, Ryan?"

@ryanlols: YES! i'm back!!!
@ryanlols: i don't know why tho
@ryanlols: i thought you'd already tried saying you wanted to be yourself in the chat room?

Tom nodded. "I did. But I forgot that the program

prioritises the most popular requests in the chat room. So, when I tried it, Grimmf had too many subs for it to work. Whereas THIS time it was the only request, and it overrode the no switch-back rule!"

> **@ryanlols:** the medicine worked because I quarantined myself!

"That's a good way to think of it," said Tom. "Anyway, I've scratched the instructions nice and big into the wall, so that everyone else who ends up back as Grimmf knows what to do. Okay, here goes, wish me luck!"

Tom typed something and pressed enter.

> **@GrimmfOfficial:** I want to be myself.

The stream ended abruptly. Ryan, Lily, and Ishaan exchanged nervous glances.

"How do we know if it worked?" asked Ryan.

Before Lily could answer, Grimmf's channel launched into another livestream. A baffled Grimmf peered at the monitor.

Ryan typed in the chat room.

@ryanlols: Nikki?

"How did you know?" Grimmf said, amazed.

@ryanlols: I'm one of Tom's friends. He wrote something on the wall for you.

Grimmf's classic charismatic grin crawled across their face as they read the message. Their eyes filled with tears.

Thank you, they mouthed.

They typed something out and pressed enter.

@GrimmfOfficial: I want to be myself.

The stream ended.

CHAPTER 38

With the reversal process underway and still giddy from exhaustion and excitement, Ryan, Lily and Ishaan skipped into the kitchen for breakfast.

"Good morning, Dad! Mmm, smells great!" Ryan said, wrapping his arms around his dad's waist.

"Don't! I'm carrying hot things!" said his dad, holding a saucepan as far away as he could from Ryan's head. "But thank you. Now go and sit down!"

Ryan kissed his mum on the head as he joined her and the others at the table. "Morning, Mum!"

His mum giggled. "Good morning, Ryan! I take it you slept well?"

"Nope!"

His mum frowned, but before she could ask him why, a plate of toast and a pot of slop was placed in front of her.

"Scrambled eggs with spinach and kale!" Ryan's dad chimed. "Help yourselves!"

Having faced a potential lifetime without food, Ryan gobbled up the green egg mush with enthusiasm – much to his parents' amazement.

Ishaan elbowed Lily. "Did you find it?" he whispered.

"Oh yeah!" said Lily.

She excused herself from the table and ran upstairs. When she returned, something floppy was in her hand.

"I managed to save this before the bins went out," said Lily. She slid a stinky old sock across the table.

"WILLY WORMINGTON!!!" Ryan cheered.

"Can you please put your Willy away while we're eating, Ryan?" asked his dad.

Ryan immediately apologised and shoved the toy under the table.

Impressed with his new respectful behaviour, Ryan's

mum made an announcement. "Your father and I had a chat last night. We've noticed how appreciative you've been, so we think it's time we gave this back." His mum held out his phone.

Ryan looked at it nervously.

"Don't worry, I wiped all the bra germs off it," his mum reassured. "But we're keeping the parental controls on your account until you're old enough to decide what things you might want to keep private."

Ryan tentatively slipped the phone into his pocket. "Thanks, Mum. I think I might take a break from streaming, anyway."

"Okay, who are you and what have you done with Ryan?" his mum quipped.

Ryan normally hated it when his mum tried to banter with him. But that morning, farts could have come out of her mouth, and he still would've savoured every moment.

"At least you have your spark back. You were very

helpful this weekend, but something seemed to be a bit off. I wasn't sure if you were getting sick," said his dad.

"Uh, let's just say I wasn't really feeling myself," said Ryan. He flashed a knowing look at Lily and Ishaan. "But I'm better now."

CHAPTER 39

Ryan and Lily waited outside while Ishaan ran into his home to fetch his school bag.

"I wonder if any other famous streamers are just advanced bots?" said Ryan.

Lily considered it as she paced around him. "Possibly."

"And is it JUST streamers? Or are there brain-hacking bots on ALL social media platforms? How would we know?" asked Ryan.

"Easy. If their life seems too good to be true, they're probably a bot," said Lily. She turned to circle Ryan in the opposite direction. "Can you hear chirping?"

"Oops! Thanks for the reminder!" Ryan said.

He pulled a jar out of his bag.

"Oh no! I forgot about the cricket!" said Lily, mortified.

"He's all right, I checked," Ryan said casually.

He twisted the lid off the jar. Lily's mouth fell open as the cricket hopped out and up his arm.

"Stay calm …" she instructed.

"I'm okay," said Ryan.

The cricket perched on his shoulder.

"Off you go, little buddy," Ryan whispered.

The cricket obediently hopped off his shoulder and into a nearby bush.

"That was INCREDIBLE!" Lily marvelled.

Ryan shrugged. "I think once you've been covered in them, one seems a lot less scary."

"Yeah, just don't try to kiss any. I can't always be there to save your life!" teased Lily.

"Pfft, you LOVE saving my life!" scoffed Ryan. "You were all, 'Oh Ryan! You're the best brother in the whole world! Here, let me sacrifice myself for you!'

It was kinda embarrassing!"

"Hah! What about YOU? 'Ooooh Lily! I don't want to lose you! Waaahhhh!!!' That's how YOU sounded!"

The siblings were still playfully bickering when Ishaan emerged from his home in a frenzy.

"You're not gonna BELIEVE THIS! Mum just got a call from her work. You know that girl in the hospital? The one who's been unresponsive for three years? She just woke up!!!"

"Oh, cool. I bet her family are happy," said Ryan, as he and Lily started walking.

Ishaan danced about alongside him. "No – think about it! She's been asleep for THREE YEARS … And Grimmf's channel's been going for THREE YEARS … What if she was the first person who had their brain hacked? What if she was Patient Zero??"

Lily gasped. "Ryan! Check your phone! See if people are still swapping back with Grimmf!"

Ryan retrieved it from his pocket and the three

walked in a huddle as they gawped at the screen.

Written in capital letters across Grimmf's inactive channel was a message …

CATCH ME IF YOU CAN!

"What do you think it means?!" Ishaan asked, alarmed.

"I think it means …"

Ryan suddenly stuck out his arms and brought them all to an abrupt halt. He pointed at the MASSIVE fresh dog poo on the footpath he'd saved them from.

"… we should focus on what's in front of us."

ACKNOWLEDGEMENTS

This account couldn't have been written without the guidance I received from Polly Lyall Grant (my constructive and considerate editor), Genevieve Herr (the sharp-eyed and curious copyeditor), or Gavin J Innes (my talented and patient partner in paranormal investigation). I must also thank Stef Keegan, Tom Goodliffe, Michael Hill, Tony Hill, Sue Hill, John Robertson, Matt Parker and everyone else who spent countless hours on the phone with me as I tried to unravel this story. Huge props to Lynne Manning and the rest of the team at Hachette Children's, Claire Nightingale (my confidant and agent at PBJ), and Berat Pekmezci (whose cover art never fails to blow me away). Finally, I'd like to thank Ryan and Lily Hay, who let me borrow their names so that the siblings this book is based on can remain anonymous.